"The spirit of Fitzgerald is strong in this one. It's a great read."

Kenny Chan
Former Senior Merchandising and Store Director,
Books Kinokuniya, Asia Pacific

"Adam Tie has a flair for characters and dialogue. Like a bite of popiah, this novel is sweet, salty and Singaporean, all wrapped up in an amusing style."

Adrian Tan
The Teenage Textbook and *The Teenage Workbook*

"*This Life Electric* is a novel about the worlds that we leave and re-enter in hopes of gaining a better understanding of where we belong. Through a wry and gently humorous narrative, Tie gives us a fresh experience of the lives of individuals trying to make their fortunes and find meaning in the dazzling, ever-changing landscape of Singapore."

Balli Kaur Jaswal
Erotic Stories for Punjabi Widows and
The Unlikely Adventures of the Shergill Sisters

T0347455

THIS LIFE ELECTRIC

Cover illustration: Tiffany Lovage

Published by LANDMARK BOOKS PTE LTD
5001, Beach Road, #02-73/74, Singapore 199588

ISBN 978-981-14-7804-8
Printed in Singapore

THIS LIFE ELECTRIC

The Ballad of The Haven

Adam Tie

◇LANDM△RK◇BOOKS◇

To Joyce, my older sister

Acknowledgements

There are so many people that I'd like to thank for making this story come to life. Thank you to my sisters, you two know me and lift me up better than anyone in the world. Thank you to my dad, you're my hero and you probably don't even realise the full extent. Thank you to my mom, you're the reason why I fell in love with storytelling in the first place.

Thanks to my editor and publisher Eck Kheng for your kindness and patience – and also for not bursting out laughing when I foolishly told you that I'd finish the manuscript within six months.

Thanks to everyone who helped inspire this book in ways you probably didn't even realise. If you flip through the pages and wonder to yourself, "hey, this sounds kind of familiar," you're probably right. If you know you know. Thank you to *cheezles, gor, bear, wolfie, doremon, the couture chasers, the safe space, nutella panther, tiny, the wolf of north east, awkward turtle, how about a be an, hoodie, jelly & ginseng, dragon, mister fffssshhh,* and of course, *mochi.*

Finally a huge thank you to you, the one reading this book. Thank you for taking the time to delve into this story. I'm one of the lucky ones.

I want to contribute to the sounds of this city
with its potent blend of logic and magic,
its mystery that rises up
into a sky that resembles the sea.
I feel its shifting weight
like the turning of tides,
young dreamer in a broken sleep
learning new ways to survive.
Awake and ruminating,
aching and breathing,
I'm one of the lucky ones,
so don't misinterpret my journey
as anything but a triumph.
Guided by strange symmetries
away with journey's end
I find myself
elevated and empowered by
all I dare to lean on –
Because when this city goes dark
and life gets heavy
Know that it is you
who helps me
carry the light.

"Airports are full of the hopeful and heartbroken."

I cannot describe Donny in a sentence. Too many adjectives come to mind. His personality bursts at the seams, refusing to be summarised and contained. The man is a force of nature. Okay, there you go. Donny is a force of nature. But that doesn't exactly sum him up either.

He has a curious gift for reading people and knowing the perfect thing to say. He takes pride in his ability to charm, to win favour and gain the trust of everyone he meets. People open up to him about their triumphs, secret joys and personal sorrows, sometimes without him even having to say a word. Donny listens as though you are the only person in the world who matters, effortlessly taking on the role of a kindred spirit, soaking in every minute detail.

We meet after nearly a decade. It is in Melbourne. I am having an afternoon drink all by my lonesome at a bar by the Yarra River just a few minutes' walk from where I used to work. Donny approaches with his trademark grin. He is in a loud floral shirt with sleeves rolled up, blazer slung over an arm, his once jet-black hair now dyed a bright brown.

"My God, you still frown like you've got the world on your shoulders," he says as he claps me fondly on the shoulder. He takes the seat next to me like he knows I am not expecting company. "I tried reaching out but I couldn't find you anywhere on social media."

"Hello, Donny."

We went to the same secondary school in Singapore but were from entirely different worlds. I frequented empty recess tables and window seats in the back of classrooms. Sometimes my classmates forgot I was even there. Donny, on the other hand, made his presence felt. When he walked into a room, the surge of energy was almost visible. If you hooked him up to a generator to convert the laughter he evoked into electricity, I'd bet that he would have powered a city.

He was like lightning, skinny and bright, close to never striking the same place twice. He did not have an entourage of friends. He enjoyed being the social nomad, adaptable and finding home everywhere.

I remember the first time we spoke. In Secondary 2, we sat just a couple of seats apart, but never said a word to each other for the entire first month of school. Then one day, during lunchtime, he sat down next to me and started a conversation.

I did not know how to react. He was loud, slightly obnoxious yet effortlessly charismatic. And before I knew it, the two of us were bonding.

I won't go so far as to call him a friend – our wavelengths were too different. We conversed in English but barely spoke the same language. Donny was used to hearty banter and people turning into his personal laugh track. I could not provide that for him. Perhaps he saw me as a challenge. He used to wait till I was drinking something before dropping a punch line just to see if I would snort water from my nose. He never succeeded but he was undeterred.

Every Wednesday after dismissal, the two of us would go hang out at his house to play PlayStation. He lived in a bungalow with a gym, garden and koi pond. His bedroom was bigger than the living room of our flat. His chef would cook lunch for us. My favourite was baked pizza because Donny let me choose the toppings.

"What's your poison?" Donny asks, signalling the waiter over.

"I'm done for the day," I say. I am halfway through my third pint and can feel the ground below me begin to shift.

"Why introduce such negativity to our reunion?" he scolds me.

"I limit myself to three drinks in one sitting. Anything more tips me over."

"Limitations are boring," he says and places his order.

Donny is in town to close a deal for his family business. He does not elaborate so I do not probe. Even when we were teenagers, Donny was private about his family affairs.

The waiter returns with a bottle of gin, cans of tonic water, cups of sliced cucumbers and lime, and a bucket of ice. Ignoring my protests, Donny begins preparing gin and tonics for us. I cannot help but notice that he keeps me in his line of vision as he mixes the drinks.

"You're still doing that thing, Donny."

"Doing what?"

"Trying to figure out what I'm thinking."

"Well, you were always difficult to read."

He drops slices of lime and cucumber into our stirred cocktails and hands one to me.

We clink glasses. After a slurp, Donny says without hesitation, "I'm sorry that you're having a bad day."

I do not respond.

He shrugs like he's merely guessing, as though he has not read me. But I know him better than that. "It's just a feeling," he replies. "I'm sorry that you've lost your job."

15

He's right, but I say nothing. Perhaps the fact that I am drinking in the middle of a workday is a dead giveaway but I am not going to invite further invasion of privacy. Donny has an uncontrollable urge to be an antidote to the poisons of life. I try to hide behind my G&T as he keeps his eyes on me.

Three years ago, my girlfriend Andrea started a creative agency. I was her first hire. We made a good team. She handled the clients while I managed their online campaigns. It was a relatively easy job because all brands followed the same structure regardless of what they were selling. Hello potential customer, here are my amazing products, here is a photo of our relatable selves, here's a #throwbackthursday, here's a manufactured behind-the-scenes shot and here is my wellspring of satisfied customers. For someone with an aversion to social media, I'm surprisingly good at it. At my peak, I was running twelve different brands concurrently.

Fast forward to this morning at 9 am sharp. Andrea and the shareholders sat me down and told me that my services were no longer required.

Jason the human moneybag did most of the talking. He told me not to take their decision personally, but it was difficult to take his words objectively given his relationship with my girlfriend.

She cried throughout the meeting, asking me repeatedly if I was okay. It was a strange question. I had no answer. So I stayed silent and accepted the outcome. When we shook hands during our parting, I could feel her hand tremble ever so slightly in mine.

I have not said a word, but a smile is on my old classmate's lips.

"Lucky you," he says. "I have the solution."

Then he tells me about The Haven.

He calls it The Haven because he truly believes that it is

one. Donny describes his place as though it is a person with tendencies, hopes and dreams. The Haven is a temperamental soul, he says. It is warm, welcoming and just a tad eccentric. It is open to anyone who seeks shelter, a drink and true connections with people from all walks of life.

In the three years that Donny has lived in The Haven, he has housed and hosted an assortment of fascinating people: ex-lawyer seeking greener pastures, pregnant teen and her boyfriend, actor running from his emotionally abusive manager, and so forth. Everyone who walked in was just a little bit lost and infinitely interesting. It was there that they somehow found their way.

I am a wary person by nature, but I feel inexplicably drawn to the concept. Something about Donny's description makes me want to experience it first-hand.

"I have not stepped foot in Singapore for over seven years."

"Interesting trivia. I'm not asking you to relocate. This is an invitation. Stay with me for a couple of days, weeks, months, or however long you decide. You look like you could use some distraction."

He picks up his drink and downs it in one mouthful. He sits back, an arm over the back of his chair, and smiles.

"There are many –" Donny continues but stops in mid-sentence. A song had begun to play at the bar and he must have noticed the change in my expression.

The universe is mocking me. I have not heard this song for quite some time. That it is playing now almost makes me laugh out loud. Donny tilts his head towards me. "You like this song, huh? I recognise it. What's it called again?"

"It's 'Love and Happiness' by Al Green."

"You must know it well then, to recognise it two bars into the intro."

I shrug and say, "I haven't heard it in seven years."

*

Till this moment, I cannot pinpoint what ultimately convinced me to come here. But here I am, thousands of miles away from my Melbourne apartment in the back of a Comfort taxi.

As soon as I switch my phone back on, there is a message from my mother typed with caps locked. It was foolish of me to assume that the note I left on my bed was sufficient explanation.

"BED EMPTY. SON GONE. BREAKFAST UNEATEN. CALL ME WHEN YOU SEE THIS SO THAT I KNOW YOU ARE STILL BREATHING."

I sigh and reply with a voice message. "I'm breathing."

"That's good to know, bro," the cab driver says.

The address Donny gave me brings me through a heritage-rich neighbourhood of shophouses, some looking worn with chipped paint and others gentrified. The taxi drives past a Thai restaurant, a French café, a bridal gown boutique, a co-working space, an ice-cream shop, a massage parlour and a duck rice restaurant with carcasses hanging in the window and uncles sitting in shorts and singlets smoking cigarettes outside on the five-foot-way.

There, in the heart of the district, is this three-storey building painted indigo blue with ornamental plasterwork in the palest yellow, lacquered windows and pop art lanterns hanging in front of the entrance. Washed in the glow of the morning light, the building looks like an oasis.

The reddest Porsche I have ever seen is parked there and leaning on it is Donny dressed in a floral shirt, charcoal jeans held up by a Ferragamo belt. His eyes are shielded by Tom Fords.

As the taxi rolls up, a grin fills Donny's face. He looks

triumphant. As soon as I step out of the cab he pulls me into a hug. His cologne enfolds me.

"I knew you'd make the trip. Do you know why?"

"Because of your million-dollar smile?"

"Billion-dollar smile," he says, correcting me. "It's because you know that you deserve a true experience, the truest experience divorced from the mundane."

"And this is the place to find it?"

"This is the place to find whatever you want, my friend," he says. "Welcome to The Haven."

"Baggage can be metaphorical.
My apartment has too much old.
I'm back looking for new."

I do not hide how impressed I am by The Haven's interior when we enter. Donny had clearly hired a top designer, then got wickedly drunk and added playful personal touches clearly meant to disarm and raise eyebrows.

The shophouse is an intriguing blend of wood, stone, copper and chaos.

At the door are a welcoming pair of Roman statues pointing dramatically up at the high ceiling where the light fixtures are halos with exposed candle-shaped bulbs. They look like crowns. There is an entire wall filled with different types of antique clocks, a grand piano spray painted with graffiti, and a pillar coloured by lipstick marks. In the distance, through French doors, I spy a pool fringed by lush greenery, beanbags and lounge chairs.

"I see that you realise that you've just struck gold," Donny says with arms inscribing a circle about him.

He ushers me past an open-concept kitchen up a staircase with a knight in neon armour at the landing to the second floor where there is a corridor with three doors.

A man with a bowl of cereal in hand shuffles out of the nearest door, walking as though he is on the verge of falling asleep. He looks about my age, but the dark circles under his eyes, patchy facial hair and curious dress sense disguise it. He gives me a slight wave.

"Are you him?" he asks, his voice a mellow drawl with barely any modulation, the exact opposite of Donny's.

"Yes he is," Donny answers for me.

My potential housemate surveys me for a second before nodding. "You have a nice air about you. The last one felt too pungent. Almost sinister. But I guess that's what makes good poetry."

Donny gestures to the shabbily dressed individual. "This is Lucien. I call him Lucy for short. He has been staying with me for over a year now."

Lucien has a languid smile. "Did you just fly in?"

"Yes, he did. Hence the baggage."

"We all carry baggage," says Lucien, directing his words at me. "It's internal for the most part. We're just waiting for those who dare to look closer." Then he peers. "It's always a pleasure to meet a Baskerville. Did you know that your – "

Donny interrupts. "Let's show him his room."

Donny swings the middle door open. It is a minimalist room with black ceiling and carpet, white walls, a bed with black bedframe and white sheets, a white table with a black art deco lamp, and a white wardrobe with black handles. It looks nothing like my apartment.

Lucien chortles. "Feels like you're sleeping inside a giant Oreo, doesn't it?"

I ask Donny if the last bedroom is his.

Lucien shakes his head, pointing to the metal spiral staircase leading to the third floor. I peer upward and see a floor-to-ceiling sliding door with a sign that reads "KNOCK BEFORE ENTERING."

"That's Donny's," mumbles Lucien through a mouthful of cereal.

"So who's the third housemate?"

"Quinn," Donny replies. "Fondly known as Madam Mischief. She moved in about six months ago and is fitting in nicely. You'll like her."

Her stay began as a one-night stand after one of The Haven's many parties. It was not with Donny nor Lucien. Rather, one of her photography subjects – a young French model who was in town for a weekend shoot. To avoid another confrontation with her traditional father about her proclivities, she asked Donny if she could take the spare bedroom for a night. It just so happened to be the day after the actress who had the room went back to her hometown of Batu Pahat.

"I cooked for them the morning after," Lucien recalls happily. "I'm exceptional at making breakfast food."

As her career ascended, Quinn's opportunity to bed beautiful woman increased. Eventually she was bringing girls back to The Haven so often that it only made sense for her to move in rather than treat it as a bed and breakfast.

"Stay with us for as long as you like," Donny says, patting me on the back.

"I appreciate that. But I won't stay for long."

"That's what everyone says."

Lucien grabs my luggage.

I look at Donny and Lucien's welcoming faces and cannot help but feel some excitement. I should expect nothing less from characters like Donny and Lucien, an old schoolmate and the strange stranger, and this curious house that seems to have a soul of its own.

"Champagne isn't detrimental to toilet bowls, but that seems a tad unnecessary."

Sometimes I feel like the old Windows screensaver. Do you remember during school lectures, how the teacher would display class notes on presentation slides? At some point of the lesson, perhaps when the teacher spent particularly long on a slide and had forgotten to turn off the auto-screensaver, the screen would go to black and an icon would pop up and begin bouncing around all four sides of the screen.

People in the class would then wonder quietly if this bouncing icon could ever fit properly into one of the corners. But it's a blue moon when it does. So many times it comes close to fitting in, before it hits one of the edges of the screen and bounces out again.

That's how I feel most of the time.

In the afternoon, as I am settling into the room, Lucien shuffles in, a bunch of clothes hangers in hand.

"Are you making yourself at home?" he asks.

I nod.

"I ask that because your luggage is still unpacked. I thought you might want to hang your clothes up."

I thank him as he places the hangers on my bed. I notice that he has changed; a stark contrast to our initial meeting. He's now in slim fit trousers and a shirt with designs of tigers riding skateboards. A cardigan is draped over his shoulders. He notices my observation and after less than a second of eye contact I look away. But I see that his eyes remain fixed on me.

"Donny showed me your work," he finally says. "I enjoy your eye for detail. Your portfolio is colourful, bright and unforgettable. You obviously put a lot of thought into what you do because each Instagram profile that you manage tells a coherent story. Every square seems to connect with each other in design, colour filter and text. Your captions are witty and poignant too, which surprised me. Your real life persona hides your humour tremendously well."

...Thank you?

"I'm a graphic designer myself." He shrugs the cardigan off his shoulder and slowly puts it on. "So, while you probably see people as an endless scroll of frames and filters, I see them as typefaces – each with unique personalities shifting back and forth in search for alignment and symmetry. That's why I find you familiar. We've never met before but I recognise you. Do you know why?"

I have absolutely no idea.

"We come from the same typeface. We're introverts in a bold setting."

My bewildered silence seems to validate his statement as he smiles to himself. "So anyway, I'm heading out for a meeting with a client, a large F&B chain. I'm going to see if they would like to extend my retainer."

"Good luck," I say.

"Good luck to you too. Donny was the one who introduced me to the client so if the contract gets renewed, we'll be partying with him tonight. And as the newest addition to The Haven, you're invited."

"I appreciate that, but I don't like parties."

Lucien laughs till his head is thrown back. He laughs slowly. "Ha. Ha, aha. Aha. Well, you're in the wrong household, then. Donny lives for it."

*

Lucien closes the deal. As promised, the client reserved a table at Velvetta, his go-to nightclub and Donny insists that I join. With reluctance, I agree. It seems impolite to refuse given how Donny has given me a room rent-free.

He and Lucien are heading out for dinner before going to the party, so I tell them that I will meet them at the club.

I put on black T-shirt and jeans and flag a taxi from outside The Haven. A cheery, bearded man greets me as I enter the cab filled with loud, upbeat and catchy Tamil music. "Greetings, young man, where do you need to go to and what is your name? There are sweets and charging cables in the back."

I tell him where I'm going and my name. The interaction should have ended there. But he lowers the music dramatically and turns around with a broad smile. Then he makes a pun out of my name and maintains the grin and the silence.

I cannot find anything in me to respond, regardless of how adorable this routine is.

"I'm not turning back around until you smile," he says.

I feel kidnapped, so I pay a forced grin. He accepts it, laughs and turns around to face the road. "There might be a jam on the way there. You partying?"

I do not reply.

"It's been many years since I went partying. My friends and I used to hit up the disco all the time."

Did you just say disco?

He stops at a red light and turns round. "You have a

magnificent name. People christened with it are generous souls and incredible humans. I knew someone with your name who donated half a million dollars to charity every year. Anonymously. I found out one day by chance. He denied it but I knew him too well. I knew he was lying."

I brace myself for an impending request for a tip. But he carries on, now telling me the symbolism behind my name. There is evident joy in his voice every time he says my name. He tells me that it reflects an attractive and bright personality, like a spotlight in a room full of fused light bulbs. I almost laugh out loud at the inaccuracy.

He segues back to his friend whom he lost to lung cancer a year ago. The man used to smoke at least a pack a day he says. The two of them would find time every week to sit down together at a 24-hour coffee shop and talk till daylight.

We pull up at the club to the sight of a buzzed crowd laughing loudly and smoking cigarettes. The cab driver takes my money and turns to me with that same broad grin, raising his hand for a high-five. He seems adamant about not giving me my change until I return the gesture, so I high-five him awkwardly. Once again, the transaction should end here. But it doesn't. His smile softens under his magnificent beard.

"I haven't said his name for a long time," he says. "I did not realise how much I missed saying it. Thank you for giving me the opportunity. I hope you will have a good night."

As I get out of the car, I cannot help but think that the pun the cab driver made with my name was a regular greeting he used for his old friend. The way he waited for me to laugh, however forced it was, seemed like the response he was used to and missed terribly.

I make myself sad weaving this narrative in my head as I watch his taxi disappear into the stream of traffic on the road, just another vehicle in the sea of taillights.

*

I find Donny at the entrance of Velvetta having a cigarette with someone. I did not know that Donny smoked. From his body language, I assume that his smoking companion is Lucien's client. The man is wearing a red SUPREME sweatshirt, a balloon crown on his head and sunglasses over his eyes despite it nearing midnight.

Donny sees me, gestures me over and makes introductions. I am right. The client catches my eye and leers in a way that makes me realise instantly that this will be an unpleasant evening. He reeks of smoke and whiskey. When he speaks, it comes out in a slur, the words fighting to find vowels.

"Bro... you like DOM?"

I have no idea who that is. Donny reads my mind. "He means Dom Perignon," he says, bemused. "Champagne. Baller Brandon is on a bigshot bender."

"I don't bend. I flex man!" Brandon says, flicking his cigarette at a nearby car. Donny roars with laughter as though the man just told the world's first knock-knock joke. "You Donny's bro?"

"Both brother and friend," Donny says. "You should consider having him manage your social media platforms. He's an absolute wizard."

The man assaults me with a punch to my chest. "Good. Good. You are now my bro. I opening 50 DOMs. What you want on the sign? You choose, I put."

I still have no idea what the intoxicated man is talking about. But as Brandon shifts to his table in the club, his flex becomes clear. When the clock strikes 12, a parade of beautiful women in body-hugging dresses, holding aloft bottles of champagne with sparklers attached to them, make their way through the crowd. One of the girls is holding an LED signboard with the words BIG BALLER BRANDON shining brightly on it.

I am not with Brandon's group. I am watching from a comfortable distance near the bar. Brandon's table is crowded with well-dressed men and women, a bathtub filled with ice in front of them. He is standing on the table, hands raised like a conjurer, drawing the bottle babes over. The men and women at the table have their phones out, excitedly taking videos and wefies of the festivities. The champagne girls circle the table, bright lipsticked smiles on their faces. Brandon's table looks like a birthday cake. It is crass but still a spectacle. The girls place the bottles, sparklers and all, in the bathtub. The ice reflects the fireworks.

Brandon snatches a bottle from a girl, shakes it, pops the cork and unceremoniously sprays the champagne all over Donny. Donny does not back away. He tilts his head with his tongue stuck out as though tasting stars.

"Good evening," Lucien says, appearing by my shoulder. I jump. "Do you know how much a Dom is worth in this establishment?"

I, as a matter of fact, do not.

"$600 per pop. Priced so high to generate plastic prestige. Brandon once went to the toilet and poured a bottle into each of the urinals. He thinks that such ridiculous acts would earn him Donny's respect. He doesn't realise that our friend is playing along because he pities him."

I watch Donny, drenched and laughing, posing for a photo with Brandon and his entourage.

"BIG BALLER BRANDON AND THE CHILLI SAUCE PRINCE!" Brandon bellows in Donny's face, making him flinch.

"That's a strange nickname," I wonder aloud.

"That's an oversimplification, but yes, Donny's family sells chilli sauce," Lucien says. "I thought you guys were close."

"He never talks about his family."

Lucien nods knowingly. "Embarrassed of the silver spoon. How very Donny."

The festivities are not over. 10 bottles down, 40 more to go. The room is pulsating as theatrical fog blasts down from the ceiling. The DJ lets out a holler. Lasers bisect every part of the club. More girls emerge from the smoke and beams of light in their tight dresses and set smiles, waving more bottles of champagne in their upraised hands, crowding around Brandon. "BUBBLES FOR MY BILLIONS!" he yells. The table erupts in cheers.

"That's factually incorrect," Lucien says. "He's a multi-millionaire at best. But the flashing lights blind us, no?"

I need to get out of here. I prepare an excuse for myself but before I say a word, Lucien points me to the exit with a toss of his head. I keep walking and breathe a sigh of relief when I reach the entrance.

I stand on the roadside waiting for a taxi. One appears but I let a group of girls take it. They hoist their friend with her skirt hiked all the way up and dry vomit hanging from her hair into it and speed off.

I notice sweat stains on my shirt like a world map. I wait, ignoring the impending headache. Another cab finally comes.

In the front seat next to the driver is his wife, tenderly stroking the back of his neck. She turns and gives me a cheeky wink. "Got no girl to accompany you tonight ah, boy?"

I ignore her giggles, fasten my seatbelt, and tell her husband my destination.

We drive off, the sounds of loud laughter and drunken yells fading away behind me.

"Don't tell me that this is coincidence, it looks an awful lot like fate to me."

The taxi takes me to the space that I know as paradise. A respite amidst grass and concrete. I tell the driver to stop and I alight at the car park entrance of HBD residential blocks. The cab driver's wife is still chuckling to herself as they drive off. Perhaps she was amused by the way I answered her questions about my personal life.

"Yes." My accent is strange because I lived abroad for the past seven years.

"No." I have never petted a kangaroo.

"27." But then again, time is a construct.

"Yes." You could say that *ang mo* women are attractive.

"No." I do not have a girlfriend and I don't want to meet your niece.

"No." I don't know a cheap supplier of abalone.

I make my way up a walkway where there are park benches every couple of steps. I walk past the first two before reaching the one underneath a giant banyan tree, a few steps away from the void deck.

I can smell the nostalgia. Everything is exactly the same as it was seven years ago. I don't know why a part of me was worried that this particular bench might have been uprooted and replaced with a frame to hang banners advertising community events, so I am filled with relief when I see it. Yet I am dismayed. Someone is on it. Sitting with one leg on the bench, the muscular individual is talking loudly on his phone. He sounds drunk and smells sour, his shirt stained and crumpled.

"Babee, no, I am not drunk. I'm fine. I'm fine. I want you to listen to me – she was, she was, just one time, okay? Just one time – I'M NOT DRUNK. LISTEN. LISTEN TO ME. I WANT YOU TO STILL LOVE ME. CAN OR NOT? PLEASE. DO YOU LOVE ME? ANSWER ME NOW. DO YOU LOVE ME?"

It appears that she does not, responding swiftly to his impassioned speech with a dial tone. Shaking the phone violently, the man lets out a cry like a wounded beast. He launches into an impressive string of Hokkien expletives before storming off.

I brace myself before sitting down. I touch the bench. It feels both cool and warm to my fingertips. In this centre of the universe, I cannot help but smile.

"I'm back," I say to no one.

This metal park bench painted green with chipping rust has meaning for me. Its setting is inconsequential. Take it out of this HDB precinct and put it by the beach, in the middle of a crowded mall, on an open grassy field, or a barren island in the middle of the sea. Whatever surrounds it, everything will blur and ebb away, losing form and importance.

There is nothing particularly beautiful about this bench. Nothing special that draws attention and captivates. But it is significant to me. It has an almost tangible significance.

I sit here for quite some time. My breath begins to steady. I glance down at my watch. It is ten minutes to three.

I stand and walk a few steps forward when something happens. The wind changes direction and the temperature shifts – the world is quiet. There is a faint smell of passionfruit.

I feel my throat go dry. The young woman next to me eclipses everything. The name that I could not say for the longest time – the one that I had lost the right to say – is caught in the back of my throat. The silence is too much to bear.

"Zephyr," I finally whisper. My voice and heart crack at the sound and she recognises the effort.

Her eyes are watery, looking at me in a way that no one has looked at me in the longest time.

"Hey Will," she says.

No one has ever managed to say my name the way she does. There is a curious way that she pronounces it, with her own distinctive cadence and rhythm that belongs to her almost as much as it belongs to me. She makes it sound beautiful. She makes it sound like a song.

In the cab ride here, the driver's wife multi-tasked – interrogating me on my life in Melbourne, stroking her husband's neck and fiddling with the radio. It appeared that she was looking for a song that moved her. Finally, after what seemed like forever, her fingers let go of the stereo knob. She had found the perfect song, her attention immediately shifting to the music. The moment it played, a curious joy charged the car.

The cab driver, who had been stoically silent the entire journey, began humming along, rapping his fingers on the steering wheel. His partner was not quite so reserved, swaying in her seat, as though it took everything in her willpower not to get up and dance. At the chorus, with its melody of percussion, piano and strings, she caught the rhythm and sang backup vocals.

As for myself – I was brought to someplace faraway. I remembered it, recognised it, but could not pinpoint exactly where I had heard it or what made it so special. But it was soothing, warm, and I found myself bobbing along, smiling, like the others in the car.

The song had Zephyr written all over it. I would have named the song after her.

"You're home," she says to me, her voice leaving her lips like a chorus.

"Everything that I have experienced in these laſt seven years had you in it. You've always been there. I juſt felt I had no right to do anything about it."

Zephyr. This woman. The woman.

For the longest time, I suspected that she was harbouring a secret. She had a superpower. She could stop time. Whatever the setting, her surroundings always needed a moment to adjust to her presence. Raindrops and birds froze in mid-air, rustling trees and honking cars and loud conversations went immediately mute as everything and everyone paused as she defied the laws of physics.

Zephyr is smiling at me now.

She is dressed in her pyjamas with no makeup on. I can see the small breakout of pimples on her forehead but she remains flawless to me.

She dries her eyes with the back of her hand, then pulls out a cigarette and places it between her lips. As she lights up, she inclines her head towards our park bench. "What are you doing here? Were you guarding the palace?"

This was where we first met. I remember it was during Mid-Autumn Festival because of Auntie Aida's decorations. Auntie Aida was my neighbour, a portly middle-aged woman with horn-rimmed spectacles and a bird's nest of a hairdo. She made it a habit every Chinese New Year and Mid-Autumn Festival to decorate the corridor of our HDB floor with colourful lanterns, faux bamboo and floral installations.

I was walking into the lift as Auntie Aida was returning home, dressed in a jade green pantsuit, a box of mooncakes in hand. She insisted that I take a mooncake before letting me pass. So, I made my way downstairs to the void deck, chewing mooncake, the lotus paste sticking to the top of my mouth.

I was fifteen. My parents and I were still living together in our old apartment. I left the house because my parents were at it again. Their arguments were always a spectacle of contrasts. My mother was a wildly expressive and loud woman. It was not difficult to trigger an argument with her and my father seemed to take sadistic joy in doing that at every opportunity. During their fights he would be deadly calm, his voice lowering to a whisper, which only infuriated my mother even more.

When they argued he would never take his eyes off her. He fixed his eyes on her as though she was prey, stretching his silence before attacking with the most deliberate, brutal words. The moment my mother snapped and started throwing things, he would allow a hint of triumph to surface as though her reaction was what he had wanted all along.

That particular evening, my father had said something in response to my mother's outburst, ever so casually, sounding almost like a compliment. I did not understand the subtext but I could tell that it was meant to do more than get under her skin; it was meant to tear through an artery. She let out a howl, picked up a pomelo and threw it at him. He ducked and it bounced off our kitchen wall. That was when I made my exit.

When I got to the void deck, there was a group of old uncles at my usual table, laughing loudly over canned beers and peanuts. So I walked further, across the street, to find a park bench to sit on. No sooner had I made myself comfortable when someone joined me.

She was in a cheongsam, her hair tied up in a neat bun. Her skin was beautiful, fair to the point of porcelain. She placed a cigarette between her lips, peach from lipstick, and lit it, blowing out a thin stream of smoke. Then she saw that I was staring. When our eyes met, I quickly looked away.

"I'll be gone after this cigarette," she said.

I glanced at the empty park benches in the stretch and she took notice. Zephyr always notices everything, even from the very beginning. "This is my favourite bench. It's hidden under this giant tree so the chances of relatives catching me smoking are slim to none."

I nodded. I did not know what else to do. She offered me a cigarette and I shook my head. I did not know why my heart was beating, beating, beating.

She unbuttoned the top collar of her cheongsam with a groan. "My parents insisted that I wear this tonight. I guess they wanted my grandparents to see me looking feminine. Pretty silly, right?"

I nodded again and she smiled witheringly.

"You're a quiet one, aren't you? If I'm making you uncomfortable, I can move to another bench."

I did not know why, but I did not want her to leave. I offered my half-eaten mooncake to her and her eyes widened with surprise. Then the two of us burst out laughing. I laughed so hard that tears flowed and my ribs ached.

Zephyr lived just across the road from my block. I discovered that if I craned my neck out from the kitchen window, the stretch of park benches below her apartment could be seen clearly in the sun and moonlight.

That park bench became ours. Some nights we would sit there for hours, talking about everything under the moon. I loved her voice. I loved the air that she carried around her. It was only in this space that I ever allowed myself to be emotional. Sometimes I'd be sitting with her and I would glance at her eyes, then her lips.

Zephyr was my safe space, at our park bench, at the spot where nothing else mattered. I thought that was all I needed. But then, one day, as with all good things, something changed.

It happened at home. It shattered everything beyond repair. My mother decided to leave. Not just leave the house, or the area, but the country. On the day I completed my national service, my mother told me she was leaving and was never coming back. She left it to me to choose what to do. I decided to follow her.

When I told Zephyr that night, she was crestfallen. In her hands was a box of cookies she had baked to congratulate me for finishing army. I could not imagine how her expression could be more painful until I told her that I was leaving in a week.

"You know what we can do?" she tried to say brightly. "We can make a day out of it. We can go to the zoo and laugh at the animals, we can catch a foreign film and ignore the subtitles, we can have dinner at that pasta place you love and then I can send you off at the airport."

I fell silent.

"I'll save the entire day for you."

I did not reply. Her smile began to wane. "Please tell me when you're leaving, I want to spend the day with you before you go. Can you let me know when you find out? Please?"

That was the last time I saw her before I left for Melbourne.

I still remember the hopeful smile on her face. I remember her hugging me tightly before I made my way back home. I remember my heart hammering against my ribs a week later as I loaded my suitcase into the taxi as fast as I could, afraid that Zephyr would catch me from across the street. Before I knew it, I was on a plane with my mother headed to Australia to begin my strange new life.

Now here we are, seven years later. I wait for Zephyr to speak but she maintains the deafening silence, gazing at me intently. I should say something. The burden that I have carried with me all these years should amount to something. I open my mouth but then I meet her eyes and remain mute.

Zephyr points to my throat, shaking her head with a wry grin. "You just swallowed. Your bad habit when holding back words remains unchanged. Kehehehe."

She still laughs in that way that is both adorable and threatening.

"Did you get my cards?"

Zephyr wrote a card to me every year on my birthday without fail. She had found my mother on Facebook and asked for our address. There was the same message in every card. The address of the park bench, and her sign off: *In case the electric eel ever comes home, you know where to find me.*

She cups her palms on my face. "You've lost weight. I wish we took a photo together so we can make a comparison."

"Your eye bags are as bad as ever," she continues. "Are you still sleeping at odd hours like when we were teenagers? No chance you've picked up smoking, have you? I hate to sound like a bad influence, but I've always wanted us to share a cigarette."

I'd tried before. It was the night when I missed her so much that I went to the convenience store and picked up a pack of her smokes. I took a few puffs, stubbed it and gave the cigarettes to a homeless man. The taste was horrible though the smell had traces of memories. But it was not enough to bring Zephyr near.

Zephyr is done with her cigarette. She hesitates. It appears that she is considering whether to leave or light up another.

I don't want her to leave. I want her to stay. She shifts on the bench, whether to adjust herself or to get up I am unsure, but it makes me panic nonetheless and I finally blurt out, "I got your cards. I kept every single one of them. And now I'm here."

She beams at me. "And now you're here."

The silence feels more comforting this time.

"How long are you back for?"

"I don't know."

"Are you just saying that?"

She is calm, but the jovialness in her eyes is replaced by a cold look that is her attempt to mask resentment. I can tell. I feel ashamed to sit with her so casually, aware of the gaping distance.

I want to say: I'm sorry, Zephyr, but do not.

"You haven't changed one bit, electric eel," she says, brushing away the irritation she so often refuses to acknowledge. She forces a smile painfully. "Still using silence to escape from feeling."

"Funny how you talk about her so dismissively but we've been discussing her for the past hour now."

I am greeted by the smell of bacon, the sound of sizzling food and a juice maker's roaring buzz when I return to The Haven. There is a terrifying amount of pancakes on the kitchen table.

Lucien is cooking up a storm, simultaneously working four pans frying bacon, caramelising bananas, flipping eggs and braising mushrooms while juicing oranges, apples, tomatoes, celery, pineapples and berries.

"Welcome back, sunshine," Donny says. He is at the kitchen island watching Lucien work his culinary magic. "Did you have a fun night?"

"Yes, thank you. Sorry for leaving early."

"You're forgiven. I'm aware that socialising is not your thing, but please don't leave a party that early again without at least a poor excuse."

He meets my eye and does not look away till I nod. He smiles.

Lucien holds up a spatula. "Would you like some breakfast? Nothing in this world is quite as wondrous as breakfast food."

"Lucy, give me your attention."

"You have a healthy 70 percent of it," he says, pouring a glass of juice and placing it in front of me. I take a sip of the fresh blend of apple, orange and celery. It is delicious.

"You were telling me about *morethanfourleafclover*," continues Donny.

"Oh yes," Lucien says, pouring pancake batter into a frying pan. "As I was saying, I've been following her Instagram page for years and so I know that she posts something every day."

"As most influencers do," Donny nods. He is looking at the Instagram profile of a young woman on his iPad. "Wow, I didn't know that she had so many followers."

"Well, it's been six months since her last update. Even when she shows up at events like product launches or food tastings, she maintains the digital silence. I think something happened to her."

That is hardly Greek tragedy. But Donny looks thoughtful.

"That's interesting," he says, a smile surfacing on his lips. "Singapore's most popular influencer has gone off the grid."

"Was that pun intentional?" Lucien says.

Donny rubs his hands together excitedly after checking another iPad for his work schedule. "Good news, I don't have any business trips this month. I'd like to invite her to The Haven's next party. Looks like she needs some help."

"Yup, someone else for you to save," Lucien says. "Shall we get Madam Mischief on it? She told me that they're friends."

"I'm sorry," I say to Lucien, pointing to the frying pan of sizzling bacon. "Could I –"

"You want to know how The Haven comes into play," Donny booms delightedly, clapping his hands together.

Lucien hands me a plate and scoops bacon on it. I grab a couple of pancakes off the tower on the table.

Donny begins talking about the unforgettable nights at The Haven – parties of extravagance and indulgence that keys everyone up for the next one. They are so much more than just nights of booze and dancing. They are experiences. At each party, conversations between his eclectic guests would resonate and impact. A Versace model from Taiwan sharing inside stories with influencers, a circle of chefs discussing the newest ethnic ingredient, a stage actor improvising a sketch with a comedian, people from all walks of life converging and conversing about all things interesting. There is something stimulating about the place and company that makes things happen.

"Whatever she's burdened with, she'll find her release here," Donny says. "That's The Haven's promise."

"Madam Mischief just replied," Lucien says, looking at his phone while preparing yet another batch of pancakes. Donny looks up hopefully. "She says that the both of them are invited to a fashion gala this evening. Consider the invitation extended."

Donny stops mid-bite into a caramelised banana. "I'll prepare the *morethanfourleafclover* party to perfection. We need to elevate."

"More than we already do?"

"Did I stutter, Lucy?"

"You never do, Don, and I credit your infallible showmanship for that."

Donny winks at me. "You came at the right time, my friend," he says. "I'm going to show you what a real party looks like. Learn to just relax and enjoy it."

Now the sound of animated laughter comes from the doorway. A group of three women and four men enter the kitchen, shake hands with, hug or air-kiss Lucien and Donny. They continue to chatter as they help themselves to the food.

One of them stands out with his bright purple hair, printed shirt of sharks shooting machine guns and olive-green shorts. He extends a hand to me. "We haven't met before. I'm Chong."

"Oh, forgive me," says Donny, gesturing to the strangers

in the room. "This is Chong, the famous YouTuber. He does comedy sketches and has over a million subscribers. The one helping herself to juice is Eileen from *Vogue*, and that's Michella from *The Straits Times*. Mikey Boy and Alex from 91.3FM radio are talking to Lucien and that's Jax who can beatbox as easily as breathing. Ronda is the owner of a vegetarian restaurant – we've all come to terms with that – ".

Donny is interrupted by the dramatic entrance of a fifth man. He's handsome, muscular and wears a smirk.

The stranger walks straight to Donny and shakes his hand. "Hi, I'm Isaac."

There seems to be a magnetic field around him – which is unnerving. Jax introduces him as a fashion model and watch dealer. It does not surprise me.

"Also a Supernova Casanova, but he's only paid in attention for that," Jax adds while stuffing his face with eggs and bacon.

"You want to try taking breaths between bites, my friend?" Donny says.

"I can't let good food go to waste," Jax answers.

"Oh, it's going to your waist, alright."

There is a burst of laughter like gunfire from the other side of the kitchen. Donny tunes in, "What's so funny?"

One of the radio DJs nudges Michella cheekily as the other guests exchange mischievous looks. She rolls her eyes. "I was just telling them about how much I hate attention-seeking bitches," she says and Eileen gives a knowing nod.

"Not so loud," Donny murmurs. "Chong is right here."

"That's pretty harsh, Michella," Chong says. "I happen to know Caroline Yum personally and she's a delight."

"Oh sure, she's the perfect girl next door. If your house is next to a mental asylum."

"Who is Caroline Yum?" I ask Lucien, a little louder than usual so that he can hear me over the sound of sizzling bacon.

The rest of the room hears me. They turn in astonishment.

Lucien stops drizzling maple syrup over a plate of pancakes well-decorated with blueberries, strawberries and whipped cream. "We were just talking about her. Caroline aka *morethanfourleafclover* is the most enchanting creature in the city," he says. "And yes, that includes the Merlion."

"You just lost Michella's respect, bro," Jax swallows the bacon that filled his cheeks and interjects, spluttering.

"I never knew I had it in the first place," Lucien says, looking genuinely surprised.

Donny uses an iPad on the kitchen island to show me Caroline's Instagram page. She has over half a million followers and her feed is an endless stream of images with beautiful aesthetics, bright colours and vibrant backdrops. Up front and centre of all of them is Caroline, beaming like the world is hers. I see the reason for Lucien's glowing testimonial. She is beautiful to the point of being ethereal. Her average likes and comments are consistent, more than any lifestyle brand and F&B company in the history of my clientele. As a brand herself, she is impeccable.

Michella rolls her eyes at me. "And another young man gets entranced by the airhead with great tits."

Alex cuts in. "Give the girl more credit, honey. I know that it seems like she has an IQ lower than her waistline but trust me, I've interviewed her and had a coffee with her afterwards. It's an act. May I point out that she has a double degree in business management and zoology? Received a scholarship, started a successful online blogshop and negotiated a prime retail space as a first-time entrepreneur. She's a hustler playing deer in the headlights."

"Are you in love with her too?" Lucien asks him.

"It's not the airhead act that bothers me," Michella says.

"Is it because she posts every detail of her life on Instagram

Live?" Elieen says, and Michella groans loudly. "What was it called again? #PickForMeWednesdays?"

"#DecideForMeWednesdays," Lucien corrects her.

Eileen notices my puzzled look and explains. "Every Wednesday, she posts polls for her followers to decide what she does. She gives them two options. Should I eat cereal or toast for breakfast? Which necklace should I wear? Should I wear a blue or pink dress today? Should I pig out for lunch or eat a salad?"

"It's a lack of substance disguised as a lack of filter," Michella says. "But no, it's not that."

"To the girl's credit, it skyrocketed her popularity," Ronda says, taking a glass of celery and apple juice from Lucien. "Brands use her for market analysis of their customers. There was even an article which named her Singapore's most honest person."

"So why do you hate her so much?" Lucien presses Michella.

"Hate is a strong word," she shoots back. "Yah, I hate her because of what happened at this beauty brand's product launch supported by *Straits Times* recently. We pulled all the stops. I'm talking portrait artists, a poet writing on the spot, caviar canapés, truffled beef, lobster sliders and gift bags worth $1000."

"What happened? No show?"

"Worse. She came but refused to post about it. Even when the organiser asked her to do a #DecideForMeWednesdays with their new product line, she refused."

"Why?"

"How the hell should I know? No explanation, just giggling and frolicking around in her cutesy way. I wanted to barf."

Donny has not said a word. I can see the gears turning in his head as he follows the conversation.

"Caroline is nothing," Isaac proclaims authoritatively.

"Uh oh," Chong says. "She's not one of your long list of ex-flings, is she?"

Isaac snorts loudly. "A lion does not celebrate intimacy with sheep."

Donny sucks in air through clenched teeth and whispers to Chong, "You can almost smell the sour grapes."

"You know what?" Chong says seriously, "I think you're right."

My eyes are transfixed on Caroline as Lucien opens one of her video blogs. She has a well-practised charm. It is different from Donny's. Even when eating breakfast, he is constantly animated, tossing a fruit or gesticulating wildly. While Donny sells himself as an entertainer, Caroline presents herself as a doe-eyed, bubbly girl facing all the wonderful new things in the world.

Isaac pours vodka into his orange juice. "I've never met her before but she's the close friend of one of my ex-flings. Apparently she has every man falling heads over heels in her wake. But she's nothing special. At least not for someone like me. I can see she's fake."

"Looks like you're not just a pretty face, Isaac," Michella says, following his lead and pouring vodka into her own glass of juice.

"I break hearts. I'd love to see her try and pull her bubbly bullshit with me. I'll destroy her, but not before I charm her. I'm a man of zero shame."

"The fact that you can say something like that with a straight face proves it," Chong says, as the others chuckle.

This talk about Caroline does not fade. Everyone has his or her own theory about her from personal experiences or gossip. Each opinion and story is fuel for another.

Donny picks up his fork and knife and digs into his pancakes.

"I love breakfast," he says, smiling to himself.

"Guests of honour never show up on time, do they?"

Later that afternoon, Donny arranges a meeting for me with a bar owner who wants to outsource the social media management of his establishment. The man has a thick Singlish accent and a warm disposition, pulling me into a hug when I attempt a handshake. As awkward as I am from the get-go, he accepts my quotation right away.

"Donny recommend you," he says, stopping me as I try to show him my portfolio. "Good enough for me lah. You're on man."

After accepting the job, I hail a taxi to return to The Haven. When I tell the taxi driver the address, he turns around and says, "Too early to go party lah."

"Huh?"

"You're going to the giant blue shophouse, right? The one next to the famous duck rice place?"

"Yes."

"If not party you go there for what?"

Eager for him to get moving, I reply his inquisition quickly.

"Oh, meeting your friend. Your friend is the owner ah? I heard that his family owns the whole row of shophouses in the area. His surname is Liang, right?"

I answer his question.

"That area used to be super quiet at night until that rich man's son came. Your friend, lah. They're the chilli sauce empire family, right? Peter Liang?"

Donny never told me anything about his family so I have no answer for the taxi uncle.

"Now that area is like circus on weekend! After midnight there is always taxis queuing up to pick up drunk passengers. That big house is famous for havoc parties. You see for yourself."

Well, if you start driving, sir, maybe someday I will.

*

During the weekend, The Haven comes to life. I finally witness one of its famous parties. It is not what I expected. I assumed that it would be like Wednesday's experience at the nightclub, excessively loud and dark with inebriated characters in every corner popping bottles and flashing extravagance.

This is different. It feels intimate yet larger than life. The moment night falls, it is as though a switch had been turned on to transform the house into something else entirely. The light of the lanterns cast mysterious shadows on the blue walls of The Haven, hauntingly so; I can imagine how beautiful it must look from afar. People drive up in expensive cars, stepping out in stylish, eye-catching outfits. They enter The Haven like it is their respite from the ordinary.

When midnight comes, the house is filled. The music is brilliant; even I cannot help but tap my foot to the beat. People dance and sway to jazz played live, tables are filled and stairways jammed with people in conversation, some deep, others loud. Waiters balancing trays of fine food or glasses of spirits and wine weave through the crowd.

I squeeze my way through bright, animated expressions

and loud laughter as the inhabitants build up the energy of the room. Nobody seems to be a stranger here, conversation struck up and celebration shared at the first hint of connection. There is not a single person in sight standing alone or fidgeting with their phone.

I catch Donny's eye and he gestures me over.

"Well, my friend, has this party exceeded your imagination?" he asks as I approach. With him is a muscular man with a tremendous beard, a dark-skinned young beauty under his arm and twins with matching sultry features. Curled up in an armchair nearby is a gentleman in a tuxedo T-shirt nestling a glass of whiskey, obviously drunk.

"This is the best party that I've ever been to," I say as I shake hands with his guests, and the twins concur loudly. Granted, I had not been to many, but this pleases Donny.

"The best party that you've been to so far," he says. "Next weekend will make tonight look like mahjong with the relatives."

"You've been saying that all night," the Irish strongman says.

Donny introduces him and the other around us. "Patrick is one of the biggest whiskey distributors in South East Asia, and Peggy, his friend, is a social entrepreneur. Barbara is the head of Singapore's top PR agency, and as though God wasn't unfair enough to the rest of the female population, that's Clover her twin sister, ex-lawyer now yoga instructor."

"And me," says the man in the tux T-shirt loudly, raising his glass towards Patrick. "I'm the one who buys half of his stock!"

After the group's laughter subsides, Donny tells me that the man is Gan Lung, owner of over twenty bars and nightclubs in Singapore, Kuala Lumpur and Bali. "He owns Velvetta, the club we went to with Brandon," adds Donny.

Gan Lung lets out a snort. "Brandon is a joker."

"Untrue. Jokers are actually funny," Patrick says and he coughs on his whiskey. I take a seat next to Donny as the group turns their attention back to him immediately. "Stop being irritating, Don. Tell us about what you're planning next week."

"Oh, I can't do that. A magician never reveals his secrets."

"Tell that to Roy and Wei Liang, they've been swapping trade secrets for the last hour."

"That's the power of The Haven."

"Pat bet Donny that he couldn't make those two alakazam guys reveal the secrets to their signature tricks," Peggy coos.

"How much money did he bet?" Clover smirks.

"I'm not at liberty to say," Peggy giggles.

"Ten thousand dollars is a lot of money," Patrick breathes heavily.

"Stop changing the subject!" Barbara says and Donny laughs loudly. "What's happening next week, Donny? I want you to spill! Spill right now!"

"Excellent suggestion," Gan Lung says, grabbing a single malt and sloshing the amber liquid into his glass.

"I'm putting in extra effort into next week's festivities," Donny says to his audience. "I don't want to ruin the experience – so if you want to find out, all you need to do is come down."

"You're a cruel man. Pegs and I are going to Macau next weekend," Patrick says.

"You are?" Gan Lung says in mid-yawn. "So am I."

"For real?" Peggy exclaims. "What are the chances?"

"What a coincidence," Donny says with a knowing smile.

"We should meet up," Patrick says. "You can stay at one of my hotels. Take your pick."

Donny shoots a look of warning at Patrick, but Patrick

does not notice and slaps his thigh as though some organic thought had struck him. "You know what, I was just thinking, we should – " he begins.

Donny reaches over for the whiskey and taps him on the arm subtly. Patrick stops instantly and turns to Donny who mutters "be patient," under his breath.

" – have another drink," Patrick ends up saying. "Excellent idea, Don. Would you like another, Lung?"

"I want something to eat," Gan Lung says, his head lolling from side to side.

"What would you like, my friend?" says Donny, flagging a waiter over.

"I want a steak. A medium rare sirloin – no, I want nuggets. I want lots and lots of chicken nuggets."

Peggy laughs loudly, clutching her sides. "Oh my God, you are so drunk, I should take a photo of you – "

"Get my friend a hundred chicken nuggets," Donny tells the waiter who rushed over and leaves as quickly to place the order.

"I hope the two of you have a fruitful discussion in Macau," continues Donny. "Meanwhile, back here in the Lion City, all those who show up for my party will not be let down."

Barbara leans over, gives Donny a kiss on the cheek and says expansively, "You never do! Till this day it still amazes me how you are still single."

"I'm not single," Donny laughs. "I have all of you."

*

On Sunday morning, after my first Haven party, I stumble out of bed. My head is throbbing and my ears are ringing relentlessly as I head downstairs. In the living room, I finally meet Madam Mischief. Dressed in a white T-shirt draped with a modern kimono featuring waves and koi patterns over tattered jeans, she is stretched out on a sofa like a jungle cat, talking rapidly on her cellphone. Quinn has pixie-like features.

"It's different from the usual order, doll. Donny wants to be impressive. Yes, even more than usual. Try and imagine that and then multiply it by ten. It's for about 100 people, but we need more champagne this time. Oh, and gin. The guest-of-honour loves gin. I need them delivered latest by Friday afternoon in case people show up early. Yes, beers, whiskey, mixers... the usual – sorry, I've got another call. Hit me up if anything.

"Hey, you're with Madam Mischief. Yo, Ellie! How's it... No, you can't show up at 9 pm, we've got the jazz band playing at that time. I can give you 8 pm, but with half pay alright? I don't want that either. Isn't it beautiful when we agree? I'll see you at 7.

"Yo, Madam Mischief speaking. Heya doll. I want your voice to be my ringtone. You what? You're already RSVP-ing, I like that. Of course you can bring a plus one. But I want you to drink for ten and end up in my bed. Ha! Alright, catch you.

"Madam Mischief here. Yes, come in early for sound check. As long as it's before 3 pm. 2 pm? Cool. I'll be here biting my fingernails in anticipation. See ya, love."

After about 10 minutes of this verbal acrobatics, she hangs up and lets out a breath. She takes notices of me from across the room. "You're the new housemate," she states rather than questions. "I'm Quinn. Be at the party this coming weekend."

Attending a party is the last thing that I want with the world's worst hangover, but I nod.

There is a twinkle in her eye as she looks me up and down. "Typical Donny," she murmurs.

Donny has made his entrance before I can even think of asking Quinn what she means. He is holding up two shirts. Not surprisingly, both are floral-patterned.

"Which one?" he asks Quinn. "I have a meeting with a luxury hotel owner in half an hour."

"The pink one. It suits your skin tone."

"Atta girl. Is Caroline coming?"

"Was there any doubt?" she says, and Donny looks ecstatic, clapping his hands together. "Jeanette Kim better not be invited, because if Caroline sees her, she's leaving after a cigarette and a hello."

"Of course I didn't invite her. You might as well ask me if I stuck a knife in a toaster."

"It'd explain the hairdo."

Donny turns to me with his roguish trademark wink. "Are you ready for the party of your life?"

No, never. I'm still getting over the last one.

"Silence means yes," Donny says, heading up the stairs to his bedroom. "I'll take that as enthusiasm."

"Horrible motto for a party starter," Quinn calls out to his retreating figure, before turning back to grin at me.

*

Throughout the week, strange new combinations of people congregate at The Haven. Something new is happening every time I walk out my bedroom door. It confuses me. Isn't the party on Friday? On Monday, Donny hosts a cocktail party of successful women entrepreneurs of all variants, sharing experiences and exchanging contacts. In the evening, he holds a swingers party and watches me, with a broad smile on his face, get accosted by women older than my mother. Then the next day he has a barbeque roast-off with a MasterChef winner, a celebrity chef who has flown in for the weekend, and a young man who has just taken over and modernised his father's hawker food stall.

Then on Wednesday, Donny has a roundtable discussion of challenged individuals. He invites a man who has been blind since birth, an elderly woman who suddenly lost her sense of smell at the age of 60, a middle-aged man with hyperesthesia and a young woman who went completely deaf after an accident. He hires someone to sign for her throughout the conversation.

Thursday starts with lawyers debating scholars, then a stand-up act by the famous comedian, Rumah, followed by a performance by the rap artist Roaracle, before ending with a bizarre celebration of kinks. People are expressive and wild, and I try my best to excuse myself. I have no idea why Donny is so insistent on me keeping him company, laughing loudly as a furry asks me if I would like to be her puppy.

"Are you enjoying yourself?" Donny says after he helps me reject her politely. I don't know how to answer that. He claps me on the shoulder warmly. "Because I know for certain that you aren't bored."

"I can agree with that, at least."

"Wait till tomorrow," he says. "You ain't seen nothing yet."

*

When Friday finally arrives, Donny's promise of escalation rings true and then some. As the activity across the stretch of shophouses stills with the closing of shutters and flicking off of lights, the energy at The Haven becomes all the more pronounced.

By the time the sunset fades and all that is left is darkness, the living room of the shophouse is crowded once again with bright and beautiful people. They arrive earlier than the weekend before. They must have heard Donny's promise that this night would be special.

The anticipation builds from the entrance of The Haven. The lanterns in the trees fronting the shophouse give a burnished reddish glow. A projected waterfall splashes down from the roof to the ground making a spectacular entrance to an already remarkable venue.

The foyer is lit by flickering candles in lanterns, channelling into a romantic pathway to the party area where a live band plays. Turn to the left and find guests dancing to the music or just chatting over it. Turn to the right and see faces of people clearly used to projecting dignity and power letting themselves loose for the night. And then at the centre of attention is a table stretching almost three metres long with rank after rank of shot glasses. It is here that Donny stands, a live python draped across his shoulders, welcoming guests to The Haven.

The snake elicits loud laughter or shrieks from every guest who sees it. The theatrics are used to great effect, but his grin flickers ever so slightly as though they are not the ones he means to impress. At points of the conversations, he glances at the doorway before returning his attention to the guests before him. It is clear who he is waiting for.

As the swing jazz band plays a roaring chorus filled with trumpets, percussion and keys, the doors swing open for Caroline's long-awaited entrance. She strolls in like it were her theme song.

Her attractiveness in photographs and videos is a pixilation of the magnetic quality she has in person. She is dressed in an emerald-coloured silk romper with bell-bottomed pants and takes up the space of the entire room despite her slim build. Every man turns and their gazes linger, including myself.

Donny does not excuse himself right away from his guests, one of whom has taken the python. He finishes his joke about snake eyes and the group laughs loudly and the gentleman with the python gives him a high-five. Only then does Donny excuse himself and make his way to Caroline.

Not missing a beat, Quinn walks over to the target from across the room and introduces her to the host. She only makes her exit once Donny elicits laughter from Caroline. They exchange pleasantries before he calls out to me. I see the wry smile they share, followed by the tossing of her head in silent mirth. There is an inside joke there, and I have a strange feeling that it has something to do with me. I shake her hand. She is even more beautiful up close and I find myself a little lost for breath.

"Hi, I'm Caroline. Donny tells me that you're from Melbourne," she says in a thrilling voice. "How long were you there for?"

"Seven years," I say. I'm getting a little tired of repeating this.

She cocks her head. "You don't look happy about that. Did you not enjoy your time there?"

Tip of the iceberg, ma'am.

"Here's your gin and tonic," Quinn re-enters the conversation with a drink in hand, breaking the silence like a pro.

"Ah, thank you, that's perfection."

"No, that smile of yours is perfection," Quinn says. She points to the row of shots on the table behind us. "G&T or not, come play the welcome drink game, love. No exceptions."

"Well, I'd hate to be a killjoy," Caroline says sportingly. "What's in it?"

"You don't want to know," Quinn replies.

Caroline picks up a shot glass and reads aloud the words

scribbled on it with a marker pen. "If you had to give up one of the following – good food, good music or good sex – what would you pick?"

Donny points at her. "Careful. The drink only brings you good luck if you answer truthfully."

"I only speak truth," she says cheekily. "Good food, of course. I don't think you'd meet a soul alive foolish enough to give up good sex. Am I right?"

A man standing behind her chokes on his drink and hurriedly leaves to clean himself up. Quinn picks up a shot glass and looks at it thoughtfully. "What's your favourite cheesy pick up line?" she reads.

"Ooooooh, I'm dying to hear this," Caroline says.

Quinn thinks for a minute before turning to Caroline seriously. "Alright, but I'll need a willing participant."

"My body is ready."

"I warn you, you might fall in love with me."

"Even more than I already am?" she says innocently.

Quinn takes a moment to compose herself before placing a hand on Caroline's hip. "Excuse me, miss, I've been here for five minutes, but I've noticed you for six. I was trying to figure out the perfect thing to say to you and I'm still struggling to find words. I wanted to ask if you fell down from heaven, but that's overused. I wanted to ask if you'd like to come home with me tonight, but that's too direct. Then I almost told you that you look familiar, but that would be untrue. Because your beauty is like nothing I have ever seen before."

Caroline bursts out laughing and applauds.

"That's a pick up monologue," Donny remarks.

"It's your turn, handsome," Caroline says.

Donny picks up a shot glass. He raises an eyebrow. "If your sex life could be described by a movie title, what would it be?"

"Oh God, don't say *Jaws*," Quinn says and Caroline bursts out laughing again.

"Or *Toy Story*," Caroline adds, and the two women high-five.

Donny hangs his head in comedic defeat. "*12 Years a Slave*," he says, and the two girls shriek with laughter.

When the hysterics wear down, they all turn to me and I reluctantly pick up a shot glass and read its question slowly.

"If you died and were allowed to ask the love of your life one question, what would it be?"

Caroline's beam segues into something meaningful as she keeps her gaze on me. "That's a great question…"

Donny sighs and shakes his head. "The questions were written by Lucien and me. No prize for guessing who came up with this one."

"Perhaps we should switch glasses," Quinn says, noticing Caroline's sober expression. "I'm sorry, this wasn't – "

"Oh, don't be silly!" Caroline laughs, her megawatt smile returning to her face immediately. "Let's all give this a go. It's a beautiful question."

Quinn lets out a long, low whistle. "I don't know. I might ask her to tell me about her day."

"I'd ask if I made a lasting impact," Donny says, turning to Caroline just as Quinn turns to me and we both get asked, "What would your question be?"

"Are you happy?" Caroline says just as I give the same answer in my head.

I look at her, hiding my look of surprise.

"Was that your answer too?" she says, as though she heard me. I shrug wordlessly.

Donny raises his shot glass up in the air. "Well, here's to a great night. Silence is golden, but let's make some noise."

Caroline giggles and gives him a thumbs up. She laughs a lot but that just adds to her appeal. She makes people feel like they are impressing her over and over again. We all touch glasses and toss back their contents bottoms up. The drink makes me shudder and the aftertaste lingers in my mouth as I feel an immediate buzz. Donny places the shot glass on the table and gestures to the party.

"Welcome to The Haven, Caroline," he says. "If there's anything that you want, just ask for it."

"That's a hell of a green light."

"Oh, you don't know me enough yet, but you will," Donny says. "My name's Donald. It means ruler of the world. Everything to me is a green light."

The DJ who took over the live band starts to play "Unforgettable" by French Montana and Caroline hops on the balls of her feet. "Oh my goodness, I love this song," she says brightly.

From the way Quinn and Donny look at each other, I realise that this was planned. In fact, the night is beginning to feel like it is orchestrated for Caroline alone. The drink in her hand, the music and the food on the table is catered for her enjoyment and sold off as coincidence. I wonder what else my housemates have up their sleeves, and why this woman is worth all the effort.

Quinn and Caroline make their way to the dance floor and begin to dance, earning cheers from the crowd. Donny wraps an arm around me and says. "I just fell in love with myself right then and there. Was it obvious?"

"Is today the first time you're meeting her?"

"Yes it is, my friend. Why do you ask?"

"This feels like a lot of effort for a total stranger."

Donny grins at me. "You're wondering why I'm doing this." Kind of, yeah.

"Because she's broken," he says. "And some way, somehow, The Haven will fix her."

*

Caroline stays till 3 am. She had fun. It is evident. As I suspected, everything about the night was calculated to make sure it was memorable for her and to her liking. The moment the energy dipped, even just slightly, out came something from left field that lifted the mood. A line of bartenders pulled out all the tricks in their arsenal, juggling glasses and bottles. Even fire twirlers appeared – one of them blowing a stream of flames next to Caroline, making her scream in delight. At one point she had the python around her neck as she swayed to the music.

Donny would entertain groups of other guests, but then time and again would glance at his watch and look for Caroline in the crowd. The moment he did this, something delightful happened. Then he would wait for her reaction and nod with satisfaction.

Before she leaves The Haven, Donny and Caroline exchange phone numbers. Donny insists that I join him to walk her to the entrance where the valet has her chariot waiting for her.

"Thanks for the party, Donny, this was amazing," Caroline says to him, looking breathless.

"That means a lot, coming from the most honest woman in Singapore."

Something crosses Caroline's expressions for a second, but then it's gone, like a trick of the lights. "Yeah, that's me," she says, before turning to me. She smiles. "I guess I'll see you around too, Melbourne boy."

Then without waiting for my reply, she slips into her car, shuts the door and speeds down the empty street. Donny is grinning at me, and I already know what he is going to say.

He cuffs me on the shoulder and says it: "Oh, lucky you."

"Hat tricks are what magicians pull rabbits out of, right?"

As soon as the last guest leaves The Haven, the grin that was plastered across Donny's face the entire night sags and is replaced with a grimace. He looks more tired than I have ever seen him as he shambles over to the pool area and collapses into a beanbag chair. I join him, feeling exhausted yet surprisingly awake from the night's activities.

I make a time check. 4.20 am. The party sounds that rang through the shophouse since sundown has stilled to a ghostly quiet. What is left are the remnants of the festivities. There are spilled drinks, cigarette butts, shifted furniture and confetti scattered across the floor. Donny is lying next to me – completely still with his eyes closed.

"Was it a good night?" he says suddenly, startling me.

"I thought it was," I say.

He sits upright and rubs his eyes. "But it could've been better. I just checked Caroline's Instagram. She still hasn't posted a single thing."

"You hosted a great party. You don't need her validation to know that."

Donny gives me a disappointed look. "It's not about hosting a great party," he says, shaking his head. "That's not the point of The Haven. It's supposed to be a space where people feel less alone, better about themselves. You saw Caroline tonight. She put on a great show. She flirted, drank, laughed and danced the night away. Then I made one joke about her being Singapore's most honest woman and the façade crumbled. She's hiding sorrow behind all that charm. So no, I don't need her to post a video of herself drinking champagne at The Haven, telling her followers how amazing a time she's having. I want her to post about something, anything. It could be about her car, the city lights, herself in pyjamas getting ready for bed, I couldn't care less. I just want proof that she feels less alone now. I wonder what else I could've done tonight."

"How is this your responsibility?" I ask him, confused.

Donny does not answer. He looks like he is somewhere else, far away. The strange look lingers. When he finally speaks, he is unrecognisable from the man who behaves like lights and cameras are constantly on him. "Does the name Tessa Ang ring a bell for you?" he asks.

"No clue. Was she an old girlfriend?"

"She was a girl who was a friend. I first noticed her in music class in Primary 6. We had to play the recorder – arguably the world's most useless musical instrument. On that day, Tessa forgot to bring hers. Our school makes a big deal out of it. They do everything they can to humiliate you for forgetting such a precious item. They make you face a wall at the back of the classroom until class is over, or call your parents to bring it from home, all sorts of nonsense. This one teacher, Madam Lau, was particularly vindictive. She wanted Tessa to suffer. So she made Tessa stand on a table in front of the class, hold up a pencil to mimic the finger positions of each musical note, and toot out the melody."

"That's awful."

"It should've been. But quiet and unassuming Tessa stood

up on the table and began to sing. And it was the most amazing sound. I stopped playing my instrument. Madam Lau looked astonished. Everyone in the class was in shock. She was so beautiful in that moment."

"That sounds like the beginning of a love story."

Donny adjusts himself in his beanbag. "There wasn't anything romantic between us. I was drawn to the loneliness in her voice. She didn't talk much but when she sang, I physically felt it, like she had reached out and gripped me, sobbing into my shirt. I could feel her sadness and it hurt me. I knew there and then that I wanted to do anything to heal her."

Donny has been serious for over five minutes. I almost look up at the sky in search for a blue moon.

"So, after class, I spoke to her," he continues his story. "We got along famously. We found common ground in our liking for Japanese tea –"

"At the age of 12?" I say, and he laughs.

"I can find common ground with anyone about anything. She'd come over to my home and we would drink different kinds of Japanese tea and enjoy each other's company. Tessa was not the noisiest or most reactive individual but whenever she said something, it was meaningful. Then one day something terrible happened to her. I won't go into the details, but it's something no one – let alone a primary school kid – should go through. It ended up with her having no place to live, so I asked her to stay with us."

"That was nice of you."

"It was presumptuous of me. My dad has no room in his house for strangers. He tells me that we have no space. It baffles me because our third maid could have a suite of her own. When I try to argue, he dismisses me, calling me a cowardly lion in Superman's cape."

He smiles witheringly as I take in breath. "It destroyed me to tell Tessa that she couldn't stay with us. She told me that it was alright. She said that she would live with some aunt or uncle. I never saw her again."

Donny clenches his fists as though bracing himself to punch through a brick wall. He is glowering with rage, feverish and shaking.

I search for the right words to soothe him. Before I do, he relaxes and says, "The Haven is for anyone who wants to find themselves. Call it a power trip, a faux paradise, whatever you want. I know what this place means to people. I know what it means to me so to hell with the throne. What use is a silver spoon that can't feed anyone?"

*

After Donny bids me goodnight and retreats to his bedroom, I stay nestled in the beanbag gazing at the clouds. It is a few moments later, as I watch the thinning night sky give way to daylight, that Quinn joins me. I last saw her around midnight bringing a beautiful blonde in a lilac dress up to her room.

"This might've been the most excessive one yet," Quinn says, as she kicks aside a stray high heel in her path. "I don't envy the cleaning service tomorrow."

She plonks down in the beanbag where Donny sat and takes out her vape pen. "Why aren't you in bed?"

"I was just about to head upstairs."

"Ah. Well, accompany me for a while. The girl in my room has been trying to spoon me for the past half hour so I had to get out of there."

She inhales deeply on her vape and breathes out a long stream of smoke. It smells like bubble gum and cherry. "Did you enjoy the party?" she says.

"I felt like last weekend's was better."

Quinn lets out a long, low whistle. "Never say that to Donny in this lifetime. The amount of hoops that he went through to make sure Caroline had a good time is incredible... I mean, he invited her favourite fashion designer from Korea and played it like Soo-yin was just another partygoer that Caroline bumped into. Donny went full Mozart tonight."

"Did you enjoy the party?"

Quinn picks up a stray bottle cap on the ground and tosses it at a plastic cup bobbing in the pool. It impressively drops in. "I always have fun at parties. It's the cloak and dagger beforehand that I hate. Showing up at events with a fake smile and ulterior motives, being deliberate with every word and gesture, inviting the right crop of people but having to invite those I personally dislike yet do it in a manner that is courteous.... Then there's making sure every single detail is taken care of so the party goes off without a hitch. It's exhausting."

"Then why do you do it?"

"Because I'm amazing at it," she says vaguely. "If I have to be a disappointment to my father, I may as well do it in spectacular fashion."

Her cellphone buzzes at this moment. I glance down at it and she waves her hand dismissively, as though someone had just blown smoke in her face. "It's the girl from the bedroom. I'm not a bowl of cereal; why would I ever want to be spooned?"

At her words, our cereal-loving roommate comes to my mind. "Where was Lucien tonight?" I say. It surprises me that he would miss out on the chance to meet Caroline.

"Donny told me that he had personal stuff to attend to. But he's never been much of a party person anyway. Most of the nights he just locks himself up in his room."

The phone eventually stops ringing and the screen returns to a wallpaper of Quinn kissing the cheek of a beaming middle-aged woman with a glowing birthday cake in her hands. Quinn notices me staring. "That's my mother. Beautiful, isn't she?"

"She has a nice smile."

"The best smile. She's the only woman who's ever known me."

Her thoughtful smile turns mischievous. She shifts her body in the beanbag and tilts her head backwards, looking at me from upside down. "So what do you think of the golden girl? Don't you agree that Caroline is one of those people who seems like she's constantly flirting even when sneezing or trying to stifle a yawn?"

"She's charming. I can see why Donny's intrigued."

"Oh I knew that Donny would take a shine to her. I'd be surprised if he didn't. What I've yet to figure out is why he's fascinated by you."

I hope that there is a rhetorical question in there somewhere. Quinn's eyes stay fixed on me as she sways from side to side. The longer this goes on, the more disturbing it gets.

"You seem perfectly ordinary to me, just another soft-spoken type with less drama than a cancelled Netflix subscription. But Donny only invites people to The Haven if they intrigue him. And that makes me curious about you."

I want to tell her that there's really nothing interesting about me. But she sits back upright and draws another deep breath on her vape. "So I took it on myself to observe you over the past few days just to see what the fuss is all about."

I raise an eyebrow.

"I noticed that you check your watch excessively, almost every couple of minutes without fail. You also stick to corners of the room wherever you are, as close to the exit as possible. It's as though you're planning your escape from the moment you arrive. But that still doesn't warrant a room at The Haven and so I'm stumped. What did you do to capture Donny's attention?"

"I didn't do anything special. We just haven't seen each other in a long time. I think he invited me here to catch up."

Quinn waggles her finger in the air. "Donny is the heir to Singapore's chilli sauce empire. He travels to at least a dozen countries a month and attends roughly 20 client meetings a week. In what little spare time he has, he dedicates it to this not-so-humble abode. I don't think he has time for meaningless catch ups."

"His life sounds exhausting when you put it that way."

"Precisely. Doesn't it make you wonder?"

"Wonder what?"

"Wonder why he does it? What does he have to gain from throwing all these parties, connecting like-minded strangers with each other, providing them shelter – without taking a single cent? I'm sure everyone has a theory about him. My theory is that he doesn't want his legacy to be chilli, so he created all of this to be significant on his own terms."

"You think The Haven is Donny's escape?" I say.

"No, I think it's his heartbeat," Quinn corrects me, drawing from her vape to blow smoke rings in the air.

*

The following Tuesday, Donny announces that he will be hosting poker night and a viewing party for the Manchester United versus Liverpool match to a selected group of guests. He invites Lucien, Quinn and myself to join. Both of them accept and I humbly decline, telling Donny that I am not a fan of the sport nor am I any good at poker. I was planning to roam the shophouses in the neighbourhood all by my lonesome anyway.

Donny recommends that I check out the antique store Find N Keep at the end of the stretch, that sells a wild assortment of antiquities and nostalgic collectibles like old telephones, enamelware, vinyl records and even furniture. "But don't be out for too long, or you won't make it back in time for poker," he says.

I restate my intention to stay outdoors till the game is over, and thank him once again-for the invitation.

He casually mentions that the Italian restaurant a few blocks away has amazing food and if I decide to pick up a couple of pizzas, it would not be the worst thing.

"Donny, I'm being serious, go ahead without me."

I return to the house at 8 pm sharp, three boxes of pepperoni pizza in hand.

When Donny sees me, he gives me a confident thumbs up.

"I'm glad I've persuaded you to join in," he says.

The terms 'poker night' and 'viewing party' usually bring to mind a bunch of guys with beers and bowls of chips. Not for Donny. That would be too simple, too commonplace. As always, he turned it into an event. He rented a card table covered with baize felt with poker chips, hired a croupier, a bartender and a cocktail waitress. It is excessive given the stakes we are playing for.

At around 9 pm, the guests begin to arrive. I recognise two of them as the musicians who played at The Haven a couple of nights ago. They walk through the house as though expecting applause.

Quinn shows up next in a collared shirt buttoned all the way to the top with yet another modern kimono over it, designs of cranes this time, matched with tight dress pants.

The musicians look delighted to see her, and a young woman immediately runs over and gives her a hug.

A spunky-looking lady, who introduces herself as the owner of a bar a couple of blocks away, arrives. She's trailed by a flamboyant man with curly hair dyed with a blue streak who wears a pink shirt that contrasts brilliantly with his dark skin. He is a radio DJ and sports journalist who used to play on the Singapore national soccer team. He apparently once scored a hat-trick with a twisted ankle, leading his team to a 3–0 victory. So I am told as we are introduced.

"It's called football, actually," he corrects as the others exchange amused looks. "And we say nil, not zero."

Lucien comes out of his room, still in sweatpants and cradling his usual bowl of cereal. It is as though he could sense when everyone would arrive and only came out when all the small talk and introductions were over and done with.

The night begins with Texas Hold'em. I am not very good. I get chastised for the first play that I make after an hour of folding, despite raking in the chips. Apparently I called down a turn bet of $45 against a short stack for an 18 percent probability to hit my flush draw, which is horrible pot odds and implied odds – whatever that means.

It is against Donny's musician friend, who has his guitar with him. He is laughing and playing the guitar throughout the entire hand but stops mid-strum when I reveal my cards at showdown. He looks at me like I am a wine stain on a white carpet.

I have half the mind to feign a phone call to avoid a confrontation, but the universe does me a favour. My phone rings really shrilly. I excuse myself, head to the swimming pool and answer without looking at who it is. Damn the universe.

Through grieved sobs, the woman on the other end of the

line chokes out, "Gary is mad at me again, son."

Neither my mother nor I say anything for a while. All I hear are the sounds of what's happening inside The Haven. I listen to the noise of poker chips being shuffled, beer bottles being cracked open, a cocktail being shaken and the tinkling laughter of the cocktail waitress.

My mother lets out an exaggerated sniff through the silence and I give in.

"Why is he mad at you, mom?"

"I'm so stupid, this shit always happens. I can't believe how foolish I am. I know Gary wants to kick me out of the house, I just know it. I should leave before he makes me do it to spare myself the indignity. I still have my pride, you know. A woman is nothing without her pride."

As expected, she does not even mention the fact that I left Melbourne out of the blue with nothing but a note and a voice message. I appreciate that.

"What happened?"

"I'm so stupid, so stupid, I can't believe it…"

A loud cheer comes from inside the house, followed by a roar from Donny. I turn to find him posing like Stamford Raffles over the DJ, who is hunched over with his face in his hands in shock. The others are laughing openly at their friend's misfortune.

"I should've never moved to Melbourne. I have nowhere to go…"

That's why you should stop packing your bags at every opportunity you get, Mom. A bit rich coming from me, I know.

"I'M ADRIFT AND LOST FROM ALL I KNOW!"

We go through this routine countlessly. Every week, my mother says something insensitive to her boyfriend. Then when he confronts her about it, her instinct is to leave, and it is his duty to plead for her to stay. She once called me into her room the night before a mid-term exam to mediate their argument. She was throwing her clothes into a large duffel bag and he, with an exasperated look on his face, took them out and placed them neatly on the bed. She would then pick those clothes up and throw them back into the bag, and the cycle would continue. Gary is an impressively patient man.

"I called him a sea cucumber."

Why on earth would you call the man you love a sea cucumber?

"He refuses to fire his assistant despite me telling him that she makes me uncomfortable."

"And that makes him a sea cucumber because..."

"Because he lacks a brain and a backbone."

I groan, which makes her wail even louder. I can hear her stuffing her belongings into a bag with increased ferocity. She has put the phone to speaker mode.

"You can talk these things out, Mom. Can you stop doing this every time that you –"

"Oh, Alison! I knew that you'd be at this again," comes Gary's voice from over the phone. He must have just returned home from work. "Hey there, kid."

"Hi, Gary."

"How's it feel to be back in Singapore? Your mom was very worried."

"It's fine, thank you for asking."

"Are you enjoying the hawker food?"

"It's –"

"DON'T YOU DARE TALK TO MY SON!" my mom yells so shrilly that I yank the phone away from my ear. "IN FACT, DON'T TALK TO ME EVER AGAIN!"

"You're overreacting, Alison. Put your things back in the cupboard."

"I'm not overreacting, YOU'RE OVERREACTING!"

"You're not making any sense, Ali!"

I hear the sound of the sliding door being pushed open behind me. Caroline has joined me with a cigarette in hand, a bemused expression on her face. She has a Manchester United jersey on, her hair tied up in a ponytail. Behind her, I can see Donny peering at us. Someone at the table lets out a wolf whistle.

"That doesn't sound like a pleasant phone call," she says, lighting up her cigarette deftly. Her voice is a beautiful juxtaposition to my mother's banshee screams.

"I'm sorry. My mom," I mouth.

"Don't be. I won't be long. I'm just having a portable toxin before I bankrupt the table."

"HOW CAN YOU BE SO INSENSITIVE!" my mom's voice rings out from my phone. I had attempted to muffle her, but inadvertently amplified the tirade with my cupped hand.

Gary says something.

"I'M SENSITIVE? YOU DARE CALL ME SENSITIVE?"

The line goes dead. The universe is kind, after all.

Caroline inhales and blows out a whiff of smoke away from me. But the cloud travels over. It smells familiar. She smokes the same brand as Zephyr.

"Are you up or down?" she says.

"I'm fine. I'm used to it by now. My mom always does this."

She looks surprised and laughs. "I meant are you winning or losing in the poker game?"

"Oh," I say, feeling my face go red. "I'm winning a little, but the guy strumming the guitar isn't very happy about it."

Caroline waves as though fanning away a fly. "Just compliment his hair or his latest song and he'll be grinning from ear-to-ear again. He's a simple soul. Donny told me that you're a genius at creating online content."

Surprised by the sudden change of subject, I nod mutely.

"My fashion label recently made it into retail, which is a different animal from what I am accustomed to. Do you have any tips for my social media strategy?"

"I'll need to analyse it properly before giving an informed answer," I say. She nods, still smiling at me expectantly with her doe-like expression. "But if you execute it the same way that you run your personal Instagram, you'll be just fine."

Her smile turns mischievous. "That's flattering. Did you just admit to stalking me online?"

The expression on my face makes her almost choke on her cigarette. "Breathe, dear soldier, I'm just teasing. What do you mean by that? Lots of colours, overlay shots, product videos and OOTDs?"

"Sure," I say, finding my voice again. She makes it difficult for me to keep my composure. She probably has this effect on all men. "That's standard practice. But you have something unique that goes beyond execution, something that I usually have to manufacture for clients. It's present on your personal Instagram and I think that you should duplicate it for your fashion brand. It's your vitality and earnestness. You're relatable yet out of reach, and it makes people wish they knew you. And then they convince themselves that they already do."

She nods thoughtfully before leaning in close, winking. "This is such strange flirting on your part. I hate myself that I'm charmed."

I sort of hyperventilate. I wonder if she can tell.

"I'd like to ask you for a favour and I hope that you say yes."

She waits for a response and after I bob my head, she continues.

"I'd like you to come to my next event. It's not an elaborate party like the ones that Donny throws, but I have a feeling

73

that it's something you will love. Promise me you'll swing by?"

She hands me an invitation card and I take it from her.

Caroline finishes her cigarette and stubs it out in an ashtray. We return to the living room where the poker table is loud with conversation and investment. Donny meets my eye and gives me the fastest wink in history.

"Hear ye, hear ye, I am here to destroy you all," Caroline says to the table pleasantly, making everyone burst into laughter. She hands the dealer a crisp $100 bill and gets a stack of chips in exchange. "Where shall I sit?"

"Behold, your throne," Donny says, gesturing to the empty seat next to me. The rest of the table exchange grins. Caroline makes her way over.

"You're out of position against me, white knight."

"Fortune favours the bold, milady," says Donny.

Caroline sits as the croupier deals a new hand. Looking at her cards, she says casually, "Speaking of favours, there's something I need that only you can help with, Donny."

"Oh goodness, everyone clear the room," Donny says, to a ripple of laughter. He turns to her. "And what may I help you with?"

Caroline wags a finger, smiling brightly. "Let's talk about it later. I'd hate to bore everyone with the details."

"Boring? You?" the sports journalist says. "Heaven forbid."

Donny obliges and changes the subject, but I can tell that he's quietly burning with curiosity. I have a feeling that Caroline knows it too.

The poker game comes to an end hours later. We head upstairs to the balcony where Donny has beanbags, a projector and large screen set up. As everyone chooses seats, Donny ushers me to the beanbag next to Caroline.

I struggle to stay awake during the entire match. Alcohol and pizzas are consumed and vulgarities are thrown. I find myself staring at the game clock, counting down the minutes till I can head to bed. I do not even dare to stifle a yawn in this space of fanatics. The ball is kicked back and forth endlessly and my eyelids are heavy trying to keep up. It feels like counting sheep.

When the match finally comes to an end, I excuse myself and purposely spend a long time in the bathroom to avoid saying goodbye to the guests.

When I finally emerge, Donny is in the living room with Madam Mischief paying the bartender, the cocktail waitress and poker dealer. Lucien had retreated to his room. He had been silent the entire night. Donny walks over and puts an arm around my shoulder warmly and I tell him that I'm sorry.

"What the hell are you apologising for?" he asks, to which I have no answer.

"I don't think that you hate me more than I hate myself."

The next day, Lucien and I go grocery shopping. He wants to make us home-cooked *popiah* for dinner so we head out to buy ingredients. After filling the bottom of the shopping cart with boxes of cereal for himself, Lucien and I comb the aisles for *popiah* skins, bamboo shoots, red chillies, green lettuce, beansprouts and other items that he reads off from a list.

As we walk past the chilled meat section, he stops in his tracks and begins prodding a frozen chicken leg with his finger. "I like to do this when I feel adrift," he says solemnly. "Just to remember my place at the top of the food chain."

In this moment of bizarreness, I ask him why he was so quiet last night.

"I had too much to drink earlier on," he says, his finger still pressing the chicken leg. "I've embarrassed Donny on plenty of occasions by talking to his guests while intoxicated. I'm proud of myself for not doing that last night."

"I thought that you would talk to Caroline, at the very least."

"Nah. I have no intention of getting to know her better. I'm a mercenary with my personal relationships. Love? Why should I throw that burden on someone like her?"

He goes still, suddenly looking rather miserable so I jab

the wrapped up chicken thigh next to his chicken leg with my finger. Lucien looks pleasantly surprised as we share a moment of mutual strangeness. At least, until the grumpy-looking employee passively aggressively asks us if we need any help.

"Oh, more than you know," Lucien says seriously, pushing our shopping cart to head for the cashier.

*

When I go downstairs for dinner hours later, Lucien's *popiah* feast is spread out on the kitchen island. Quinn and Donny are standing up on their chairs taking photos of the lush sight. The *popiah* skins are neatly folded into individual triangles for self-service next to Lucien's bowls of *popiah* filling: stewed bamboo shoots, plump prawns, coriander, omelette, sweet sauce, tofu, beansprouts and Chinese sausage. He proudly points me to his homemade chilli paste as we begin creating our own rolls with the ingredients.

"I know that it's not the same calibre as Donny's family recipe, but I'm very happy with how it turned out," he says.

"Nonsense," Donny says, after scooping a spoonful and tasting it. "Yours is better."

"How egregious," Quinn says, nudging him cheekily. "Why would you shame your forefathers so?"

Donny does not look remotely abashed. "I never said that our product was bad. We have a great product. We couldn't be outsold even if we tried. But a million bottles of Liang Family Chilli Sauce will never taste better than a fresh batch of homemade chilli. Do you know why?"

"Because it lacks soul?" Quinn grins.

"That and more," Donny says. "It lacks panache."

"You know what I lack?" Lucien says. "An understanding of

the word 'panache'. But I appreciate the compliment."

I overestimate the springiness of the *popiah* skin as I overstuff it and cause it to rip in the process of rolling. In shame, I scoop up the ingredients and make another, this time with two layers of skin. Quinn laughs, rapping hip-hop lyrics as she wraps a simple *popiah* of chilli, bamboo shoots and prawns. Donny is precise with his. He starts by slathering chilli and sweet sauce directly on the skin, then after piling on a healthy amount of each ingredient, wraps the *popiah* up. It swells with flavour but does not tear open like mine.

"Perfectly executed," Lucien says to him.

"Thanks, Lucy. What're everyone's plans for tonight?"

"I've got a lot of work to do. I'll probably just stay in."

"I've a date, or is it dates? Do you use the plural if you're going out with twins who both want to sleep with you?"

"I'm probably going to do work as well," I say. "I've got to schedule a photoshoot for your friend's bar."

"Really?" Donny says. "You're not going to Caroline's party?"

I meet his eye from across the table as he gives me a gentle yet stern look.

"It would be impolite of you not to show up. Do you think that she personally invites any Tom, Dick and Harry to her events?"

Lucien stops mid-bite, causing the ingredients in his *popiah* to splatter on his plate. "Caroline did what?"

"Holy shit," Quinn says, looking not at me but Donny in amazement.

I really, sincerely, would rather not go to a public event, Donny.

He smiles as though he hears me. "Caroline told me about its premise. Trust me, this is precisely the kind of event that you'd love. It's not popping bottles in a nightclub, and it's not chaos at The Haven. Some missed encounters are more regretted than others."

He delivers this with such sincerity that I turn to Lucien for help but he is still gaping at me in amazement, his *popiah* drooping in his hand.

"You're at the top of the food chain," he says.

"I'll drive you over after dinner," Donny says, proceeding to wolf down his *popiah*. "And Lucy, for God's sakes, were you poking raw meat at the grocery store again?"

*

Donny drives me to Caroline's event, as though to make sure I go. We head down in his second car, an olive-green sporty BM. He brings up the top to make sure that the hair that Quinn styled for me stays intact. She was meticulous about it, taking almost half an hour.

During the entire ride, Donny throws Caroline's accomplishments at me like darts at a dartboard, hoping to hit a bullseye.

"She's beautiful, you know. Young queen. She's stunning, magnificent, gorgeous, ravishing and alluring."

"All those words mean the same thing."

"I know – bet you'll never find another woman in her league for the rest of your life."

I'll take that bet, Donny. I'll wager it against everything that you have and can borrow.

We drive up to a coffee shop with a traditional Chinese signboard. The food stalls are all closed except for a stall selling *kopi*, *kaya* toast and steamed dumplings.

"I think that we're at the wrong place," I say.

"Nope." Donny cuts the engine of the car. "It's in a back alley that I can't drive into. Just walk past the coffee shop and go straight in all the way."

I get out of the car.

"Let me know if you need a ride home – but then you might have alternative sleeping arrangements tonight." He grins at me, his arm on the driver's window, expecting a reply. But I just stare back blankly till he rolls his eyes, winds the window up and drives off.

I walk along the alleyway, past an elderly gentleman in baggy shorts and singlet with a towel around his neck. He is clipping his toenails. As I reach the end of the road, there is a deserted park with a playground on my left, a row of shops on my right. Only one of these shops still has its lights on. It is a quaint art gallery, with people crowded outside having wine and cigarettes, chattering loudly.

I feel my fight or flight instincts kicking in. I glance at my watch. I'm on time. Caroline, dressed in an eye-catching red jumpsuit, is taking photos with a group of young women. Her practised smile brightens up and makes way for delight as she sees me. After the photo is taken, she waves animatedly in my direction.

"I'm so glad you came!" she says, hugging me tightly. She smells floral and oriental. "Can I get you a drink?"

"I'm fine," I say. She links her arm with mine and guides me into the venue.

The space is small but the installations are potent. There are Greek panels of war and decadence, sculptures of heroes and gods in glory and sorrow. In the middle of the exhibition is a blank space under a spotlight in front of a dark blue background. Above it an arc of words in pink neon reads: "No man ever steps in the same river twice, for it's not the same river and he's not the same man." Below this, hung by invisible strings from the ceiling, is a silver crown. Guests take turns posing for photos in this spot, strategically positioning themselves so that it looks like the crown sits atop their heads.

"Very Instagram-worthy," I tell Caroline. "Whose idea was it to quote Heraclitus? It's perfect for the theme."

She beams at me. "I wish I could claim credit, but I was told that it was the event organiser's idea. I have always been fascinated by mythology and ancient history. This exhibit will run for the next two months, but there's a special event tonight that I was invited to host. The organisers are not able to pay much, but when they told me the premise I could not find it in myself to decline."

"What is it?"

"You see that spot where everyone's taking selfies? Later at 9 pm, it will be the stage for whoever dares to stand on it. The audience will then call out words, anything off the top of their heads, as cues. The person on stage picks one word that resonates with them and uses it to talk about their personal experiences. Would you like to give it a shot?"

Ha. Funny. Hell no, absolutely not. I have so much no in me that I want to turn No into a double-syllable word. That is the most ridiculously terrifying thing I can possibly imagine, and my imagination is vast. Hell no, hell no, and hell to the ends of the earth ending with a no.

"No thanks."

Her hands are still holding my arm. She has not let go of me since I arrived. Whether unaware or ignoring the people looking at us, she is humming happily under her breath as we circle around the exhibit.

Caroline stretches the silence significantly before saying, "Are you familiar with the concept of demigods?"

"Yes."

"I love the concept of the Greek gods, gatekeepers and immortal, yearning for mortal souls under their rule. These overpowering desires leads to the creation of demigods like

Hercules and Achilles. Do you know why they did so? Why they acted on such impulses?"

"Because it made them feel powerful?"

The room begins to become still and quiet, everything around us ringed in a hazy blur. Caroline shakes her head, smiling achingly. "It's because they were lonely."

"Will? Is that you?"

I turn and find Zephyr standing in front of me. The room begins to move again. The waiter stilled in mid-motion continues to top up a glass. The flash of the camera phone held by a handsome man under the crown flashes. Someone taking the world's longest sip of champagne can finally set her drink on the table.

Caroline's hold on me finally loosens. Zephyr laughs and moves to wrap her arms around me. I hug Zephyr back tightly.

"Kehehehe. It really is you. What are you doing here? You hate public events."

I gesture to Caroline, who turns to Zephyr with a smile. "Hello, nice to meet you. My name's Caroline."

"Of course. Everyone knows you. I work with Yong Shen. We're the events company that hired you for this event."

"Oh! How rude of me," Caroline says, her tone shifting back to bubbly. "You guys did an amazing job. This place looks perfect! Thank you for letting me be a part of this."

"Well, the event starts in 15 minutes. I'll talk to you later then, Will." She gives me a wave.

Zephyr returns to the group she was with. Many are staring at me unflatteringly. One even scowls, boring his eyes into me. When I catch his gaze, he rolls his eyes and turns away.

"She's very pretty," Caroline remarks.

"Yes, she is," I say.

At 9 pm sharp, Caroline gets on stage to the loud applause of the crowd. You could have mistaken her as the organiser of the event. She thanks everyone for coming to the exhibition in her cheery voice that I now recognise to be perfectly practised. It is a switch that she can turn on whenever she wants. Her incredible tone soothes and thrills at the same time, keeping her audience hanging on to every word. Hate her or love her, she has you charmed from that very first second.

"Well, enough of me chattering away," she says to the laughter of the crowd. "Let's begin! Who would like to go first?"

Someone walks through the crowd to the stage. Caroline gets out of the spotlight for her to step into it. It is an exotic-looking middle-aged woman wearing a beautiful ethnic headdress. Someone shouts "spectacles". Another person yells "nail polish". Numerous other things are bellowed. It is only when someone calls out "beach" that she begins speaking.

"She's ridiculously hot," says a voice next to me and I jump. Zephyr has made her way over, two sliders on a plate in hand. She offers them to me and I take one from her.

"She has a very nice headdress."

"I mean Caroline."

Caroline is hugging the woman offstage, the both of them in conversation as the next person takes the spotlight.

"How do you know her?"

"She's one of Donny's friends."

"Donny? Geez, I didn't know you still kept in touch with that human hot air balloon."

"I'm living with him, actually."

Caroline catches my eye from across the room and gives a rippling wave with her fingers. How she managed to make that gesture look both adorable and flirtatious I have no clue.

"She likes you," Zephyr says. "Did you see the look on her

face when I approached? It was very telling."

"I think she was just threatened by your aura."

"Oh, that too, of course. Do you like her?"

A man with a charming smile is approaching Caroline. He cuts into her conversation with the woman in the headdress like it is the most natural thing in the world to do. They shake hands and she laughs coyly.

"She doesn't like me," I say.

"You reckon it's already escalated to wuuuuvvvv? Trust me. Believe it or not, I'm actually a girl. She does like you."

I'm the human equivalent to a Nokia ringtone. Who on earth would?

Zephyr smiles at me as though she heard me. "Who wouldn't like you?"

*

I excuse myself and go to the men's room as a sylph-like woman takes the spotlight. I take the last urinal of the row. As I unzip my fly, someone approaches. He picks the one right next to me, trapping me against the wall. I recognise him as Zephyr's friend who rolled his eyes at me. He continues glaring at me even as he urinates. It is a very uncomfortable experience.

"What the hell are you doing here?"

I'm trying to relieve myself. I presume you're here to stop that.

"Do you even know what you're doing?"

Have the rules of bathroom etiquette changed since the last time I was in Singapore?

He raises a hand dramatically, still scowling as he grips my shoulder tightly. "I want you to check yourself."

I want you to wash your hands.

"Zephyr is a forgiving person. She's salt of the earth. But from what she tells us about you, you know her more than anyone. So you know what she's gone through and the abandonment issues that she has."

Ignoring nature's call, I zip up my fly and flush the urinal. But he does not take the hint. He stands there glaring at me, like we're two cowboys in a saloon squaring off.

"I don't even know you and I hate your guts. You're a shitty friend. You're a piece of shit, unflushed and clogging up everything. And worst of all, you're not a man. You're a coward."

A group of laughing gents enter the toilet. But still Zephyr's friend does not flinch. His arm is still on my shoulder, scowling at me, waiting for me to speak.

"I know," I say.

Shaking his head in disgust, he turns and storms out the door.

*

"Bro, are you serious? You don't know what *ang ku kueh* is?" Zephyr's friends with slack-jawed expressions gape at me.

She had invited me for drinks after Caroline's event and I agreed. I did not know that it would be with the additional company of her friends. Her girlfriends had left for a nightclub, while Zephyr, three of her male friends and I went for drinks at a nearby bar. We get an outdoor table.

From the get-go, I feel like a turnip at a steak buffet. The three men are identically dressed in white collared shirts and black dress pants with designer belts. They look like a boy band. Paul and James introduce themselves, while the one who cornered me at the urinals begrudgingly says he's Ashley. The two work in finance, while Ashley is from the same events company as Zephyr.

Paul and James make small talk with me. Ashley lounges in his seat, watching me like prey over his whiskey.

"You don't know what *ang ku kueh* is?" Paul repeats. James, similarly slack-jawed, explains, "It's a sticky stuffed red turtle shell on a banana leaf."

"I'm sure that I've eaten it before. But I don't know the name."

"You must be bluffing," Paul shakes his head in disbelief. "Didn't you grow up here?"

"Do you know what satay is?" James says.

"Yes, I know what it is."

"How can you not know what *ang ku kueh* is then?" he says, scratching his head.

Zephyr excuses herself to go to the ladies, smiling at me apologetically as she does so.

Paul changes the subject. "What do you do again?"

"I'm a social media manager."

Ashely raises his eyebrows. "You don't seem very social."

Well, you're an events organiser but you're not very eventful.

The conversation subject changes. The dismissal is evident. There is no further interest in me. But there is an elephant in the room: everyone knows what I did to Zephyr seven years ago.

Zephyr returns to the table with a bemused expression on her face. "Are we done making snap judgments about my best friend?"

The night is over. Ashely insists on paying for Zephyr's drinks. Then, as we all get up from the table to leave, he reaches over and holds the small of her back. It is for less than a second but it seems like forever to me.

Ashely scowls when Zephyr agrees to share a taxi with me

instead of accepting a ride home in his Audi.

In the cab I ask Zephyr if Ashley is interested in her.

She rolls her eyes. "I tease the guy endlessly. Once to the point of tears, if I may add. Why would he?"

"Why wouldn't he?" I say.

**"Just look at what you've done for me,
oh pretty woman, I'm still in love with you."**

A couple of days later, Zephyr invites me to join her and her friends for trivia night. I ask if anyone from Caroline's event will be there, and she replies: "Just the guys, why?"

I reject the invitation immediately, but she tells me that one of her teammates has fallen sick and the team is in need of a fifth member. Rejecting Zephyr now feels akin to stabbing a mermaid and I lack the willpower to do it. So when the day comes, I keep my promise and head down to the postal code she sent over.

It is a hipster craft beer bar with graffiti on the walls and Edison light bulbs hanging from the ceiling. Square tables joined to form eight large rectangular ones are spaced across the venue.

As I was forewarned, Ashley is one of the team members. He is seated next to Zephyr at their table and looks crestfallen when he sees me from across the room.

James and Paul yell out "*ang ku kueh*", waving at me jovially. "Why did you invite the *chiak kantang*?" Ashley says to Zephyr. "If you were looking for a deadweight, I could've just brought the expired fire extinguisher from the office."

"Like your hairstyle, Ashley, that joke fell flat," she says to him. She hugs me and moves to sit beside me. Ashley sulks at us from across the table. "Are you pumped?" she asks me.

"Like an overinflated basketball," answers Ashley. "Thanks for inviting him."

A man in a plaid shirt and a thin moustache steps forward to the middle of the room. The quizmaster introduces himself as Xun Wei, but everyone seems to already recognise him. Xun Wei explains the rules of the game. Each table is only allowed to give one answer per question, and no cellphones are permitted. Anyone caught using their phones to google will be immediately disqualified. We are given 15 seconds of discussion time per question, after which we have to write the answer on a small whiteboard and raise it in the air when the time is up.

He gives us the thumbs up; no one has any questions. We are treating him like an air stewardess giving safety instructions before a flight.

"Alright, let's begin!" he roars. "Question one. In what year did Singapore football legend Fandi Ahmad become head coach of the Singapore Lions XII?"

Oh crud.

Ashley looks gleeful at my befuddlement as he snatches the whiteboard out of Paul's hands and begins scribbling away. When the time is up, Ashley raises the whiteboard in the air confidently.

"The answer is 2013! I want to give bonus points to those who specified that it was in December, but sorry, I can give you a high-five instead."

Ashley looks at me smugly as he shows the table that he had included the month in his answer. Then he erases the whiteboard in preparation for the next question.

I maintain silent for the questions that follow. Four of them are about Singapore pop culture, the next one is about an actor whose name I do not recognise, then a few are about some American and Korean television shows, and then finally a question about the number of Ballon d'Or awards that Leo Messi had won.

"I see there are many FC Barcelona fans in the room," the quizmaster says. "The correct answer is five Ballon d'Or awards! Well done to... yep... everyone in the room. Five questions to go!"

We are tied in third place with I Thought This Was Date Night. Ahead of us on the scoreboard is Hold My Beer and The Quizzard of Oz. Ashley fashions a piece of paper cut up like a Toblerone bar into a crown and puts it on his head. Zephyr asks him politely if he did it to stop his brain from falling out. I nearly spit out my drink.

"Next question, ladies and gents! When did the Stonewall Riots occur?" the quizmaster says.

Ashley turns to Zephyr and she spreads her hands, palms upward. For the first time all night, the two of them are stumped. Paul looks over helplessly at the next table, trying to sneak a peek at their whiteboard. He is spotted; one of the members of team SMRT Alec covers it with her hands and hisses at him.

I know about the Stonewall Riots. It was the catalyst for the LGBT civil rights movement in America. For three months, I was in charge of the Instagram page for a drag cabaret restaurant in Melbourne called Sizzle & Spice. The owner of the bar named herself Marsha after Marsha P. Johnson, and I remember her being forever proud that her birthday fell on the same day as this defining moment in an era's struggle for equality.

"June 28 1969," I say softy to the group.

I have been dead silent till this moment. James jumps as though he had forgotten that I was still at the table. The others turn to me as Zephyr takes the marker from Ashley and begins writing my answer on the whiteboard.

"Hold on, can anyone confirm this?" Ashley demands. "How do we know this is right?"

"Oh, eat a brick," Zephyr says, raising the answer in the air.

It is correct. We are now ahead of I Thought This Was Date Night and tied with Hold My Beer. The next question asks what Tiger Wood's real first name is. Ashley takes the whiteboard from Zephyr. After writing the answer, he not only raises the whiteboard in the air, he gets up to his feet with his chest puffed and waves it violently. The answer is correct, and Ashely takes a moment to bow to different parts of the room before sitting down.

We are catching up. Hold My Beer gets the answer wrong, and we jump to second place while The Quizzard of Oz is a mere point ahead of us.

"Name the brands that use these slogans," the quizmaster says. "What's the Worst that Could Happen, Every Little Helps, and The World's Local Bank."

The first answer is Dr Pepper, the second is Tesco supermarket and the third is HSBC. Before I even have the chance to tell the team, Zephyr grabs the whiteboard from Ashley's hands and passes it over to me. He looks positively furious.

Hold My Beer and The Quizzard of Oz both get it wrong. We are now in a deadlock for first place.

The next question is a tricky one. We are told to rank a list of peppers in order of heat levels. The 7 Pot Douglah, Naga Viper, Carolina Reaper and Bhut Jolokia. All five of us have different guesses, but we go with Ashley's choice because his younger sister is in the culinary field. It ends up being wrong, but other than We Is Geni-YAS, all the teams in the room get it wrong too.

"Time for the final showdown!" Xun Wei says excitedly as

the room buzzes with excitement. "The final question is... are you ready? No, that's not the question. Or is it? No, that's not the question either. But ladies and gentlemen..."

"Oh, shut up," Ashley mutters under his breath.

"Here we go! The final question is: who's the singer? I'll give you three clues and you have to tell me the name of the artiste."

Ashley groans. Clearly music is not a topic that he excels in. Zephyr and I catch each other's gaze and everything around us dulls and loses colour. Zephyr grins at me.

"Clue number one, he or she is one of the most famous soul singers of all time," the quizmaster says.

"That's good news so far," I say.

"I couldn't agree more," Zephyr's grin becomes even more pronounced.

"Yeah, me too," Ashley chimes in.

"Clue number two, he or she had a guest appearance in the television series *Ally McBeal* where he or she shows up as a vision."

Zephyr knows the answer already. I can see it on her face, clear as day. But she waits for the third clue just to be sure.

"And finally, clue number three... one of his or her albums is named *I'm Still in Love with You*. One bonus point if you can name three songs from the album – and no, the title track does not count."

There it is. I know the answer too. Zephyr and I are still looking at each other. She reaches out to pick up the marker. I place the whiteboard in front of her.

"Do you know the answer, Zeph?" Ashley says.

How very amusing. The universe is a stand-up comedian, going through its routine that has the crowd on the edge of their seats. They are loud with laughter at one moment, and then they go silent as they are presented with something profound and almost heart-breaking before being caught by surprise and howl with laughter again. They marvel at how calculated and witty the universe can be. Everyone understands its humour for the most part, but then the universe casually slips in a joke that no one seems to get. They wait eagerly for the punch line as the universe grins, microphone in hand, proud of its handiwork. It scans the room for someone, anyone, who understands and is pleasantly surprised to find two people in the audience grinning back.

Zephyr flashes me a knowing smile, and I cannot help but mirror it.

"My voice," she says with a wink.

James and Paul look at each other in confusion. Ashley is glaring at me. He has no idea what Zephyr and I have gone through together. No one at this table, or away from it for millions of miles would ever know. It is for her and me alone.

When the time is up, Zephyr raises her whiteboard up in the air. Her answer is Al Green, and she writes down three songs: "Love and Happiness", "For the Good Times" and "One of These Good Old Days". The Quizzard of Oz picks Al Green as well, but they are unable to name any songs from the album.

We win trivia night. Ashley takes off his paper crown and puts it on Zephyr's head. James and Paul hug each other enthusiastically.

"You knew too, didn't you?" Zephyr says, turning to me.

I beam at her. "Of course I did."

"Kissing you is the antidote to the chaos."

Despite the countless times that Zephyr and I met below her flat, there were only a handful of times when I went to her place on the tenth floor. She could only bring me up when no one was at home – there had to be a perfect symmetry of circumstance. It had to be a night when her mother was out playing mahjong with friends, her father was out drinking in questionable KTVs with colleagues and clients, and her brother was staying the night with his girlfriend. There was only once when she had come over to mine.

When the night was over, the two of us never spoke of it again. It was an unspoken decision we made to take it as an isolated incident that rested in its own dimension.

It started at our park bench. I remember that it was a week before I had to enlist for national service, and she was teasing me about haunted toilets, push ups and put downs and poor cookhouse food when it started pouring with rain. We did not leave right away. We stayed there talking until Zephyr's cigarette was snuffed out mid-puff. We could not go upstairs to her flat. Her mother had decided to host mahjong at home and would be playing till daylight.

I do not know what made me so bold, but I suggested that we go to my place. Zephyr looked at me in surprise.

My parents were at a family friend's birthday party, and my mother had told me that they would be out till late. The logistics made sense, but it took more than that for me to make the invitation. Zephyr recognised the gravity of my words and gave me a chance to take it back. I didn't.

"I'll do it on one condition," she said.

"You cannot smoke in my place. My mother would murder me."

"Oh, not that. I'm not so daring. I'd just like to do something for you to remember me in army."

"What would that be?"

"I would very much like to shave your head."

"Literally?"

"Yes, literally. Why would I want to metaphorically shave your head? I've shaved my brother's head and it was a pretty darn good job if I may say so myself. Can I do it? Please? Pretty please?"

So that was how the two of us ended up in my bedroom, old newspapers on the floor and a shaver in her hand. Zephyr had asked me to wait below her block as she went upstairs to get the things she needed. Ten minutes later she rejoined me with a big bag of stuff.

When we were in my bedroom, she took the items out of the bag one by one. There was a sheaf of newspapers, a shaver, two cans of beer, a scented candle, a portable vinyl player and a few records. She put the chair from my desk in the middle of the spread-out newspapers, sat me down and pointed to the mirror next to my cupboard.

"Would you like to say goodbye to your hair?"

"I was never particularly attached to it. No pun intended."

"Liar. That came out from your mouth way too naturally."

She switched the shaver on. It gave a tremendous buzzing sound. With a huge grin on her face, she edged the shaver closer and closer to my head before running it swiftly through my hair. With a whirring noise a clump of my hair fell to the floor. She shrieked like a kid who had just seen snow for the first time.

"Show some professionalism."

"Enthusiasm is professional, Will."

Another whirr of the shaver and more of my hair fell. Zephyr was laughing the entire time, and within minutes she was done. She turned off the shaver and clapped the hair off her hands, smiling at me as she admired her handiwork.

I rose to my feet. Stray hair fell to the floor as she brushed off my shoulders and pants. I looked at myself in the mirror.

"Hmm. A touch more badass, don't you think?"

"I never thought that you could look even manlier but here you are, like the billy goat gruff. Alpha male. Big daddy. Mister Supreme."

"There's playing along, and then there's patronising."

"I sensed that I took things a step too far when I called you an alpha male."

"No, you're wrong there, that was fine."

I rubbed my head, staring at the foreign look for a while as Zephyr added touches of warmth and soul to my room. She cracked opened the beer cans, lit the candle and played a vinyl on the record player. The tune was beautiful, one with trumpets and light percussion.

"Who is this singing?"

"A magician disguised as a singer. Al Green. I love him."

The room was filled with a newly warm glow and the scent of passionfruit and vanilla. She switched the lights off and sat down on my bed. "I like your room."

"You don't have to say that, Zeph. This isn't an awkward first date."

"I'm aware of that. We've already gone through the

courtship process."

"How did I do?"

"Passed with flying colours, my good sir."

At that moment, loud sounds came from the living room. Zephyr jumped to her feet. We stood there in silence, listening closely, when yelling and another crash rang out. It sounded like things being thrown against a wall. Zephyr turned to me in alarm.

"Should we call the police?" she said.

"Don't bother. I doubt my parents would appreciate you breaking up their fight."

"Your parents...?"

"You have NO RESPECT for me regardless of who is in the room!" my mother screeched. Even through closed doors, I could hear every word she said perfectly. "Who do you think you are to call me that? Did you think it was funny?"

Then my father spoke, and we could barely hear him but his voice was deadly calm as always.

"Your insecurities are amusing," he said.

"It's not about INSECURITIES, it's about RESPECT! I don't know how to look Jamie and Michael in the eye again. You made me look like a fool in front of everyone!"

"You did a perfectly fine job of that on your own."

Zephyr turned to me. "His voice brings a chill down my spine. Is that your father?"

"Yup."

"He sounds like a very scary man."

"He is."

Then he said something in a muffled voice that we could not make out, but it clearly stung because my mother let out an outraged scream. More things were thrown about.

"Does this happen often?" Zephyr said quietly.

I shook my head. "Not every night."

"YOU DO NOT KNOW HOW MUCH I HATE YOU!" my mother screamed, banging her fist against a wall. "Get out of my house now!"

"Your house? I'll get out after you…"

There were sounds of a scuffle then the slamming of a door. Silence.

Zephyr took me by the hand and sat us on the bed. She sat close to me, resting her head on my shoulder. "Tell me about your family?"

I took a sip of beer. "Do you really want to know?"

"I want to know about anything you tell me," she said.

So I began to tell her everything. I told her about the way my father was and the way my mother was. At some point, they convinced themselves that they were in love. Perhaps they were very young, or very lonely and all they had was each other. So they ended up together and I was perhaps the only reason why they stayed together. Sometimes that made me resent myself.

"What does your father do?"

"He's a lobbyist. I suppose that's why he's methodical with his insults. My mother lashes out. My father goes for the jugular. She'd be rambling on and then he'd say something like, 'look at you – always so anxious – it's no wonder why your own mother thinks you're unworthy to be a parent.'"

"Holy – that's just cruel."

"Yuh huh. There's always layers to the things he says."

Her expression softened and I looked down at my feet.

I told her about one incident that always came back to me, even though my parents had fights of higher magnitude. It was about my report card. A teacher said that I was not paying enough attention in class and had zero participation in class discussions. She said that it was as though I was mute.

My mother, furious, wanted to march down to the principal's

office and give him a piece of her mind. I was in the kitchen eating ice cream, but I may as well have not been there. They never bothered to mince their words in my presence.

"Since when is silence a sign of disobedience?" she said furiously. "Just because my son is quiet does not mean that he is not listening. How dare this man question my son's intelligence. I bet it's because his son is as smart as a bowl of fruit and talks a lot to overcompensate."

"Like you, you mean?" my father said behind his newspaper.

My mother turned her head and shouted, "And now you're making this about me? This is about our son and how his school does not understand his personality."

"Oh, it's fine if that's the case," he said. "But you are, as always, making this about yourself. And if you march down with your anger and spit, you're going to make things worse. Like you always do."

"THIS IS NOT ABOUT ME! THIS IS ABOUT OUR SON'S PROBLEM AND HOW IT'S AFFECTING HIS GRADES!"

"It is always about you. You overreact to the stupidest, smallest things. This man is doing his job. But you're angry because deep down you think there is something wrong with your boy."

"HE'S YOUR BOY TOO! STOP ALWAYS MAKING THINGS MY FAULT!"

And I stood there, taking it all in, watching them hurl insults at each other with both increasing and decreasing volume. At the end of it, my mother dragged me by the collar and drove down to the school to confront the principal. She was fighting back tears the entire ride and I remember that all I could do was repeatedly tell her I was sorry.

I did not realise that Zephyr had placed her hand over mine. Our fingers were entwined. "What your parents do to each other has nothing to do with you," she said gently.

"I know," I said. "But – "

"You're an amazing person, William," she interrupted.

I did not know what to say.

"I want you to look at me, listen to me."

She was crying a little. At that point I had yet to see her cry. It was not one of those stormy, overdramatic crying fits for the whole world to see. She was smiling at me comfortingly, but a tear was rolling down her cheek. It was one of the most heart-breaking things I had ever seen.

"You are the most wonderful soul I've ever met. And I'm lucky, grateful and honoured to be with you. And I want you to know that there is a difference between being lonely and being alone. And as long as I'm in your life, you're going to be neither."

I think it was at that point when I realised that I was in love with her. But I said nothing. Instead I lifted my right hand and brushed her tears away with my fingertips. For a while she said nothing, and then she rose to her feet, went over to the vinyl player and said, "Let's rebel against your parents' fury."

She pulled another vinyl out of its sleeve and put it on the player. Switching it on, she placed the needle on a specific track and, with a soft scratching noise, a guitar strummed, a man spoke and music began to play. The rain was absolutely pouring right now, splattering on the window as the skies let out a rumble of thunder. Zephyr was before me, swaying to the music, rocking her hips from side to side.

It was a beautiful song. Zephyr turned to smile at me and I felt my heart ache.

"You like that, huh?"

"I do. What is it?"

"'Love and Happiness'," she said, crossing the distance back to me. "The best kind of music hits you a certain way. You can't describe exactly how it makes you feel, but deep down you know it fully. Your heartbeat quickens as everything starts to slow. You know it's significant and you hold it close because it makes you feel everything. This is the song that makes me feel safe. I can't quite put to words why it makes such an impact, but it does. I feel safe here. "

"That's how I feel about you."

She looked at me in surprise. It was as though I had just told her that I loved her. But I could not string those words together no matter how much I wanted to.

"What did you just say?" she said. She was staring at me with a curious expression on her face. A sense of wonderment came over me.

There is probably a song out there that has a resounding impact on everyone who listens to it, Zephyr. Some would stop in their tracks. Some would smile. Some would break down in tears. Some would remember it from somewhere, played on a jukebox in a dive bar, or on a roadside in front of a closed mall that makes a couple break into dance. It could lift someone up. It could make the world slow. I'd name the song after you.

"I said, that's how you make me feel," I said. "I feel recognised."

She flashed me a tearful smile. "I'm your favourite song?"

That was as succinct as I could have put it. It was not what I was fully capable of verbalising, but for us it seemed just right. It stated my inclinations as best as I could with no promises, yet left no room for doubt.

"You're my favourite song," I said.

Then she kissed me. From the moment our lips hovered to the point where they touched, everything seemed to move as though we were building up to something momentous. I pulled away, suddenly anxious that we were on the precipice of ruining something sacred with something fleeting.

But then her dazzling eyes met mine and then it was my turn to lean in and kiss her beautiful face. I wanted to hold her in my arms forever.

Later when we were naked and I moved inside of her, she gripped the back of my neck and dug her nails into me. I winced as she shuddered. I could feel her warm breath against my skin and it gave me goosebumps. I felt home inside of her as she wrapped her legs around me and I caught the rhythm of the dance. Her moans were beautiful. She was beautiful. I was the luckiest guy in the world and an extra planet.

When we were finished, we lay on the floor together for what seemed like hours. The rainstorm had quelled. Zephyr and I both knew that she had to return home. She rose to her feet, the beautiful silhouette of her naked frame in the moonlight stirring and taking me over.

That was the first time we kissed and had sex. It was the only time. We never talked about it again – the next night when we met on the park bench it was like we were best friends who had not seen each other for a long time.

Fully dressed now, Zephyr bent down and kissed me on the cheek. My eyelids were heavy and I was exhausted. She stopped me from sending her to the door, smiling as she did so.

"I'll let myself out, electric eel," she whispered. "Just go to sleep. Thank you for tonight. Thank you for being you."

As she opened my bedroom door and turned one last time, I saw her give me a wave and a smile.

I did not like this feeling. It felt like goodbye.

"Long live the ice ball that dared to go rogue."

After almost a month of living in the The Haven, I am used to the unusual habits of my housemates. They are an eccentric trio, living isolated realities in a communal space.

Lucien is someone who seems perpetually on the verge of lighting up a joint. I once found him staring hard at a pear in his hand. It turned out that he had been up all night working and wanted to rest his eyes by looking at greenery.

He also has the tendency to point out the specific fonts used in anything – signs, menus, posters and greeting cards – something I noticed on the day we met. Sometimes he did it with people too.

"Hello Optima, fancy meeting you in a place like this," he would say to a total stranger. "You probably get this a lot, but you made the right decision with Meddon as the display font on your menu," he would say to a bewildered waiter waiting for us to order our food. "I can barely spell it, but Bebas Neue rolls off the tongue so beautifully and fits you perfectly," he would tell a car saleswoman handing him her name card. He once shuddered and turned away from a YouTube video Donny was showing us, saying, "I cannot respect a person who uses Comics Sans in any way that is not ironic. You might as well use Wingdings while you're at it."

Quinn is a social dragon. Whenever there are guests in the house, her presence is met with great enthusiasm. She is almost the female equivalent of Donny, entertaining and instantly likeable. Lucien is more like myself, the two of us turning into mere spectators, one-sentence responders at best as Quinn and Donny charm and engage.

I have never seen Quinn truly alone. Even when using the bathroom, she is accompanied by a lover or has someone on the other end of a phone line. Interaction seems to be her specific kind of oxygen.

She once showed me her trophy collection, a display cabinet with rows upon rows of lipsticks from bedtime conquests. It is a habit of hers. After getting attractive women into bed, Quinn makes sure to take their lipstick before they leave.

All things considered, I actually enjoy talking to Lucien and Quinn.

The three of us are having a breakfast of toast and soft-boiled eggs with pepper and soy sauce. It is one of those rare mornings that Donny is not at home.

He is not on one of his frequent flights, but instead at a spin class – a bizarre sight to imagine. Donny once told me that he refuses to exercise in the morning for one specific reason. Physical exercise takes dedication and resolve, and he refuses to waste precious willpower on something as trivial as exercising to start his day.

This makes his going to early spin class such an eyebrow-raising decision, but the three of us move on from it to talk about more interesting things.

"Is that what I think it is?" Quinn says to Lucien, pointing to his iPad's wallpaper. It is a photo taken on a traditional Japanese wooden bridge wet from rain and glowing in the evening light. A woman is walking mid-step in the centre of the bridge, a red umbrella over her head as cherry blossoms burst magnificently around her like fireworks. It is an iridescent photograph.

"Yes," Lucien says proudly, shoving the iPad under my nose like a father showing photos of his newborn to a colleague at the water cooler. "Madam Mischief was sent to Japan last year by a travel agency to cover the cherry blossom season. This still remains my favourite photograph that she has taken."

Quinn takes a long, slow puff of her vape and blows out smoke rings. "Do you know who I feel sorry for?"

"People incapable of making a proper segue?" Lucien says politely.

"Japanese weather forecasters. I'm sure you guys know that the sakura season is a big thing for tourists."

"I can imagine," Lucien says.

"Well, it's everything you think, but bigger. When I touched down in Japan, it was mayhem. You'd think Pikachu was proclaimed President or something."

"Casual racism is the best racism," Lucien says calmly.

"Thousands of tourists travel from around the world to see the blossoms. Plane tickets aren't cheap, neither are accommodations, so these visitors plan their entire schedule around the weather forecaster's calculations. The slightest error could cause thousands of people to fly out of Japan even before the first bud opens. The precision these forecasters need to predict the bloom of a wild thing is incredible."

"Exactly," Lucien says to Quinn, dipping his toast into his soft-boiled eggs. "Which is why life is like ordering *cai png*."

"We were literally just talking about poor segues, Lucy."

Lucien finishes his eggs and toast and licks the spoon clean. "If you think through the mechanics of *cai png*, it teaches you one key fact about life."

"What's *cai png*, again?" I ask.

"It's mixed rice," Quinn says patiently.

"A lot of people just point to the items that they want through the glass and then watch the *cai png* auntie pile their food up on a plate for them. Rice. Boiled cabbage. Fish cake. Grilled chicken. So on and so forth. But there is a secret art to ordering *cai png*. The common misconception is that by ordering less rice, you get more ingredients. False. The truest way to get the most food is by pausing after each item. You tell her that you want the chicken, or the pork, or whatever, and then you wait for her to finish loading food on your plate. While waiting for you to tell her the next ingredient you want, she may scoop food on your plate unnecessarily to fill the silence. Then, when you have lengthened the awkward silence long enough, you tell her your next choice."

"You're like an unsharpened pencil, Lucy; do you have a point?"

"My point is that life is about timing. With the right kind of quietness, you don't only realise what you want. You get what you want, too. There is always a necessity for silence because people are uncomfortable with it. So if you know how to work silence in your favour, whether on an empty stomach or when you're starved for intimacy, the right kind of silence gives you everything."

Lucien smiles as the two of us look at him with appraising looks. "On a related note," he adds on. "When you order *cai png*, don't order fish first, because the auntie will just think that you're a rich boy."

"You're such a beautiful weirdo," Quinn grins, inhaling deeply on her vape and exhaling a stream of coffee-smelling smoke.

On cue, Donny kicks the front door of The Haven open, dressed in activewear, sporting a bandana around his forehead. He is blasting "Soul Man" by Sam & Dave on his phone, victory dancing across his features. He greets us good morning with great news. After agreeing to go with Caroline for spin class, they had brunch together. She has asked him for a favour.

"That's such a Caroline move," Quinn grins.

"Making me do something humiliating?" Donny says as he tugs the neon-coloured headband off his head.

"I told her that you don't like exercising in the morning. I guess she wanted to see how accommodating you'd be."

Donny shakes his head mirthlessly. "The girl loves a power trip even when she's running on fumes, eh?"

Caroline still has not posted anything on Instagram, even after her spin instructor asked her to do so. It appears that her attention has been captured by a fresh endeavour. As she explained to Donny over her plate of spinach and poached eggs, she has been inspired by The Haven and Zephyr's event to organise something of her own. She wanted Donny's advice on how to reach out to people from all walks of life without needing to use her online platform. So, he offered The Haven to her as a venue and promised to help her invite interesting people.

I stare at Donny. No one should look this ecstatic from being asked for a favour.

"Why do you think that she's so adamant to not use her Instagram?" Quinn asks Donny.

"I don't know and I can't wait to find out," he says, picking up a piece of toast and taking a bite. "She seems so happy all the time. But whenever she falls silent, she gives herself away. At the centre of Caroline's bubbly nature, there is a tension."

"Did you just say attention?" Lucien says.

"He said a tension," Quinn says.

"Yes I did," Donny says.

"Okay."

*

Donny is in an exceptional mood, as though the Singaporean government decided to turn his birthday into a national holiday. He suggests that we head out for lunch and his favourite dessert, *ice kachang*.

When we reach the hawker centre, Donny tells me to get a table while they queue up for chicken wings and satay, black carrot cake and wanton noodles. It takes me a couple of minutes but through the crowd, I find a vacancy beside the drink stall. I walk over quickly and sit down.

As soon as I do that, a shadow looms over me. The woman approaches like a cowboy in a spaghetti western, removing enormous Gucci sunglasses that cover nearly her entire face.

"Ah, boy, you're sitting at my table."

"It was empty when I arrived."

"Does this..." she says dramatically, pointing down at the floor. "...mean the table is empty?" I turn to where she is pointing and see a packet of tissues near where I sit. The wind must have blown it off the table.

"Yes?"

She looks at me as though I had just admitted to being raised by wolves. Two other women arrive at the table. She has summoned backup. The three of them tower over me as I gaze, bewildered.

"I hope you are ready for the best meal of your life," comes a cheery, booming voice from beside them. Donny arrives with two bowls of wanton noodles, with Lucien carrying two plates of black carrot cake behind him. Quinn must still be queuing up for the chicken wings and satay. My housemates set the food down on the table.

"Are these friends of yours?" Lucien says good-naturedly,

gesturing to the scowling women.

"They think that I took their table."

"And how did that happen?" he says. I point to the tissue packet on the floor, expecting him to mirror my bewildered expression, but he nods. "I see."

"Your friend here has no manners," one of the aunties says. "Get off our table or else."

"Surely there's no reason for hostility on such a sunny day," Donny says. He is acting as though we are having this conversation on a yacht. The aunties look at him with confused expressions. "We did not know that this table was taken. There are three of you, and this table can seat eight. We'd love to share it with you, if you lovely ladies do not mind? We'll be out of your perfect coiffures in no time. How about a round of sugar cane juice on me?"

There is a stunned silence before the one in leopard prints declares, "I want a *kopi*."

"A *kopi* you shall get!" Donny says. "And what would the rest of you beautiful ladies like?" They giggle like girls.

Donny works his magic yet again. The tense moment is diffused. The ladies share our table. After supplying them with drinks, Donny buys each of them a packet of tissues. He even offers to share with them the giant trays of chicken wings and satay bought by Quinn.

But they still shoot daggers at me when they leave the table. My face burns with embarrassment while Donny, Quinn and Lucien happily continue to dig into the food.

"I didn't mean to do that," I mumble.

"But you did, they reacted, I fixed it, and it's fine," Donny says, stuffing his face with wantons. "Don't burden yourself with what's past."

After our meal, sweaty and parched, Donny says he'll order *ice kachang* for us. I decline. I have always thought that it is too complicated a dessert to enjoy. Ice cream, on the other hand, is simple. You know exactly what you are getting the moment you point at it through the frozen glass.

The appeal of *ice kachang* has always bewildered me. According to Zephyr, back in the 1950s, Singapore street hawkers used to sell it as a literal iceball, simply with syrup drizzled on it. Things went haywire from there.

"It's a snow cone that went rogue," Zephyr said to me once while queuing up for her favourite dessert. "Do you know what makes it special?"

"A lack of moderation?"

She flashed a withering smile. "It's a dessert of dimension. With *ice kachang*, you have to dig deep to get to the good stuff."

"You are romanticising a dessert, Zephyr."

She made a face at me.

"On the surface it just looks like syrup and evaporated milk on shaved ice. But as you eat your way through it, you taste the ingredients of jelly, red beans, *attap chee*, sweet corn, sweet potato, agar-agar and whatever strikes the hawker's fancy. It's not for everyone, but you cannot deny that it is memorable. Long live the iceball that went rogue."

"You're smiling to yourself," Lucien says to me, a melted mixture of brown liquid dripping from one corner of his mouth. "Are you off in a happier place?"

I did not even realise that I was smiling. Seeing them eat *ice kachang* makes me recall what Zephyr used to always do when eating this intimidating dessert. She would bore through, scooping red bean, jelly and *attap chee* as she ate. When she made a tunnel and the ice mountain did not collapse, her look of pure bliss never failed to make me laugh.

"Yes I am," I say.

Donny tilts the bowl of melted slush up to his lips and finishes it. "Lucky you," he says.

"Maybe I want you to say no."

"How's Zephyr?"

It's after lunch. I am back in my room in The Haven. I am on the phone with my mother. Standard procedure: she tells me about her daily grievances in a wild and expressive voice. Whether it is about getting her car scratched, losing a client, or even accidentally ordering walnuts in her salad, she always manages to make it sound like the end of the world. But then she brings up my best friend out of the blue, and I hear her tone shift. She says her name with unnecessary emphasis, like an inebriated person trying to give the password to a speakeasy bar. I do not like it. It annoys me when people are careless with Zephyr's name.

"She's good, Mom."

"I'm glad. She's a very sweet girl. She wishes me happy birthday every year without fail. I remember she used to be so naughty but I guess she grew out of it? Last time when we still lived in Singapore, I caught her smoking downstairs at a park bench. She looked so shocked when she saw me. I guess it was because it was at night and she wasn't expecting to be seen by anyone. I was walking Mrs Long's dog for her when she went overseas. Do you still remember Mrs Long? The woman with the huge mole on her chin? From level 6 or 7,

I think. It's level 6 right? Anyway, I was helping her walk her dog and when I was crossing the street I saw Zephyr smoking. Do you remember her dog's name? I think it was something edible. Like Biscuit or Cookie or something. Mrs Long was in Bali with her daughters. I think one of them used to have a crush on you. You both went to tuition class together. What subject was it for again?"

"Which of your questions would you like me to prioritise?"

"Does Zephyr still smoke?"

"Doesn't Gary smoke?"

"That's not the same, son. He's a man."

"What difference does that make?"

"Women should not smoke. It's unladylike."

Throwing things after losing an argument is also unladylike, Mom.

"I need to go, Mom. I have work to do."

"Huh? I thought you lost your job. Didn't you lose your job? Let me go see your card again – have I ever told you that your handwriting has not improved since you were in Primary school?"

"At every chance you get, Mom. I'm freelancing at the moment. A couple of Donny's business contacts are interested in my services. I've deadlines to meet, I'll talk to you later."

"Wait! Before you go, I wanted to tell you – I had a dream about the two of you. You and Zephyr."

"What was it about?"

"You know what, though? Now that I think about it, the dream was a little strange. Maybe it's best if I don't say it."

"Okay? Well, I guess in that case, I'll just –"

"We're back in our home in Singapore. I'm asleep in bed when there's this hammering on the front door. It doesn't sound like it's being knocked on with a fist. It sounds like it's being kicked. There's more sizeable impact. So I jump out of bed and open the door and there you are, a little boy, with this strange-looking flower bud cupped in your hands, tears streaming down your face. So I make you a hot Milo to try and calm you down but I keep realising that we have run out of things. First the Milo tin is empty, then I cannot find the milk, then the cups are missing and I cannot find any spoons. So I return to the living room and you're still crying over the flower bud in your hands. I ask you what's so special about it and you tell me that it's Zephyr. Your hands are clasped together so tightly, and you're crying so hard, and you keep repeating yourself, 'she's going to bloom, mom, I know she is. We just need to give her time. She's going to bloom.' And no matter what I say, you refuse to let her go. You were being such a silly little boy."

After the phone call with my mother, I head downstairs to the kitchen. Donny and Quinn are having a conversation at the island and their eyes light up when they see me. I cautiously walk to them.

Quinn is smoking her vape as always, and blows two streams of smoke out of her nostrils like a cartoon villain. She gleefully informs me, much to my bewilderment, that Caroline wants me to ask her out for dinner.

"Maybe you misunderstood the subtext," I say.

"First of all, I never misunderstand subtext. That's why I always get laid," Quinn says. "Secondly, Caroline was very upfront. The girl knows what she wants and I think you should leap at the opportunity. I'm sure that you can see that she is the apex of attractiveness. Hell, I'd date her in a hummingbird's heartbeat."

"Would you be interested?" Donny says.

"I just said that I'd date her in a – "

"I wasn't talking to you, Madam Mischief."

The two of them look at me expectantly. Recognising

my hesitation, Donny offers to pay for dinner. When I still hesitate, he compounds the offer by saying that he will lend me one of his cars. Still, I stay silent.

"Why on earth are you hesitating?" Quinn laughs.

Donny is watching me intently. I make sure to avoid his gaze but I know that even the most subtle switch in my facial expression will not slip his notice. Then he surprises me by backing away. "Madam Mischief and I are simply relaying the message. It's up to you to decide what you want to do with it."

I nod. When I make my way out of the kitchen, he calls out to me. I turn back and meet his eye. Something sincere has replaced his usual cheeky grin. "Don't keep looking back at the past, you might turn to salt," he says. "Meeting Caroline will only have two outcomes. It will either just be a dinner between two incompatible people or you might have the time of your life. What do you have to lose?"

*

I head down to the park bench later that evening where I find Zephyr having her regular 10 pm cigarette. I tell her about Donny's proposition and she does not look surprised.

"I knew that she fancied you," she says, stubbing out her cigarette on the ground. "What do you want to do?"

"I have no interest in getting into a relationship with her."

"That's not answering my question. Do you like her?"

"She's interesting. But I don't want to date her."

Zephyr lets out a whistle and lights up another cigarette. I want her to tell me not to go. I want her to tell me that it is okay to not want to go. I wait in the silence, and after a pregnant pause she turns to me and smiles. "I think that you should meet her."

"I'm surprised."

"I know you are. It's just dinner, Will. Not every action you make has to be a revolution. You're always talking about missed connections, maybe you should give this one a try. You might just have a great time."

"Do you want me to?"

"I think that there's no harm in giving it a shot. But let's not be mistaken here. If she does anything to hurt you, trust me, I will destroy her. You remember what I'm capable of. Kehehehe."

"You're talking about the fight with that girl in the car park, I'm assuming. You almost lost, by the way."

"Nonsense. I was completely in control."

Zephyr uses a finger to nudge me gently. I sway sideways before returning back to her like a pendulum.

"Do you really want me to go?" I ask.

Of course she recognises the hesitation in my voice. I can see it on her face. "It's not about what I want, electric eel. It's about what you want. Objectively speaking, that woman is a bombshell and I think your heart could use some opening up."

"I don't need anyone but you."

She smiles. "I can't be all that you have."

"Why not?"

Zephyr wraps her arms around me tightly, resting her head on my shoulder. I can feel her smile close to my chest. "Because you deserve so much more," she says.

*

When I ask Donny for Caroline's phone number, he breaks into a dance. In the background, Lucien gapes in shock and hands a crisp $50 note to Quinn, who is grinning smugly. I wait for Donny to stop flailing, which takes a moment. When he is done, he calls her phone number and gives me the phone in a theatrical manner, as though handing me the keys to the castle. After a couple of rings, Caroline's cheery voice sounds out from the other end of the line.

"You're calling me at the booty call hour, handsome. What can I help you with?"

"Er... yes."

There is a pause on the line before it transforms into her laughter. "Hi, Melbourne boy. How may I help you?" she says. There is an ever so subtle shift in her voice.

You may, actually. I do not know why I'm doing this, or why you want me to do this but you're a thrilling person and it would be nice to have a quick bite together with no expectations moving forward. Would you enjoy that?

"W-w-would you like to have dinner with me?" I say.

There is another pause over the phone. Donny is still grinning at me maniacally and I want him to stop. Quinn is taking the longest inhale on her vape imaginable. Then finally, Caroline speaks.

"I prefer being asked in person, but as expected, you defy conventions. I'd love to have dinner. Tell me the time and place and I'll be there."

When I hang up, Quinn tilts her head up and exhales a stream of smoke from her mouth like a wolf howling at the moon. Donny dashes over to Lucien and pulls him into an excited bear hug as though he had just witnessed me walking on water.

"Nostalgia is a funny thing, isn't it? It lures us into thinking that we want something more than we actually do."

I could start a bank. As soon as dinner with Caroline is confirmed, everyone wants to give me their two cents. The next day over a hearty breakfast of Lucien's homemade curry puffs and *kopi*, my housemates sit me down in the living room to dish out advice. They act as though I have never been on a date in my life.

"So what are you going to wear?" Quinn asks me, brushing curry puff crumbs off her bottom lip. "Here's a tip: Caroline likes guys who can pull off the preppy look, so I suggest you go for a tailored dress shirt over chinos with a blazer over them. Then dress shoes or loafers, depending if you want to look dressy or casual."

"Thanks, Quinn," I say. "But I think I'll just wear this."

Quinn looks at my black T-shirt and jeans. "You're joking, right?" she says.

Donny bursts out laughing at Quinn's expression of horror. "You've been around me for too long, Madam Mischief. Our friend here puts less effort into his dressing than I do."

"That's like saying there's less water in your bathtub than the ocean," she says, before turning back to me. "You're going out with the hottest girl in Singapore and you're going to wear your everyday clothes?"

117

"Yes I am," I say. From the corner of my eye, I see Lucien smile into his *kopi*.

"Which is perfectly fine," Donny interrupts, just as Quinn opens her mouth to say something. "The modern armour is relative. What matters most is that you're comfortable and you engage in hearty conversation with her. Compliment her smile, her wit, laugh at her jokes and respond to her questions."

"And what about the food situation?" Lucien says. "Should he chew it immediately or let it marinate in his mouth first with a sip of wine?"

I laugh and Quinn slaps him on the back of his head playfully. Donny cuffs me on the shoulder like he always does. "At some point of the night, she's going to decide if she's just infatuated with you or if there's symmetry. And you two have more symmetry than you think. She's close to her mother, just like you are. She's an overthinker too. I'm also willing to go out on a limb and say that you two have almost identical taste in movies and music. But at the same time, you two are also very different, which will result in either a balance or a clash. While you're stingy with your words and picky about company, she's outspoken and approachable to everyone. She documents her life for the world to see. You don't even have a Facebook account."

"You don't have Facebook?" Quinn says. "Aren't you a social media manager? That's like a pilot with airsickness."

"I have never found using it necessary to be good at my job," I say.

"Well, it helps you build connections. It's actually how I met Caroline."

"No way, you slid into her DMs?" Donny says, his lips twitching.

"Well, this was when I was still building my portfolio. I reached out to a couple of influencers asking them if I could shoot them for free, and she was the only one who replied. She was really kind about it. She made it seem like I was the one doing her a favour. At that point, I had only taken photos of friends and unaware strangers. I was really nervous."

"It's hard to imagine you nervous," I say.

"I was a wreck," Quinn says. "She told me to meet her at an event launch and if anyone asked, tell them that I was her personal photographer. So I remember borrowing a dress from a friend, putting on too much makeup, and showing up with my camera draped around my neck. There were beautiful people left right and centre and I didn't know what to do with my hands so I clutched my camera for dear life, holding it up over my face like it was a shield. Then I saw a good moment shared between socialites and took a snapshot without even thinking. It was a great photo. I gained confidence and shot another one. I kept taking photos of the crowd till I reframed and refocused, back in my element. Just as I was feeling on my A-game, Caroline showed up. Even back then, she was easily the hottest girl in the room. I did not immediately walk over, watching her walk through the crowd from afar behind my camera lens."

"Creepy," Donny and Lucien say at the same time.

"I felt the perfect moment coming. I've always been able to anticipate and capture something in its most photogenic form. It's instinct to me. So as soon as I saw Caroline walk towards her friends, the group of them unaware of her arrival, I readied myself, my finger on the shutter release button. But before Caroline caught their attention, somehow I had caught hers. She turned and looked right at me through the camera lens and I swear my entire body froze. It wasn't love

119

– it was submission. Then her friends saw her and with wild expressions they dashed over to welcome her. It would've been such a great photo if I had captured it. That's what I'll always remember Caroline for. She's the girl that made me hesitate on the shutter."

"That's one hell of a testimonial," Donny whistles as he and Quinn turn to Lucien. He is walking back to the living room with a carton of milk, a bowl with a spoon in it and a box of cereal. He notices all of us staring at him.

"Oh, don't worry, I could hear you from the fridge. Caroline's the girl who makes you ache and stutter?"

"Hesitate on the shutter," Quinn grins. "You've barely said a word this entire conversation, Lucy. Would you care to chime in?"

Lucien shakes his head slowly as he sits down. "No one ever wants unsolicited advice, it's like a teabag in a glass of whiskey. But more importantly, no one needs unsolicited advice from someone like me."

"That's not true," I say, and Donny raises his eyebrows at me. "I would love to hear what you think."

"Why?" Lucien says, looking genuinely confused.

I shrug my shoulders. "I want to hear from someone of the same typeface."

I see Lucien's face gradually break into a smile. "You're not joking?" he says.

"If I was joking, I would've asked you for fashion advice," I say and he laughs in his trademark slow way.

Donny watches the two of us in quiet fascination, as though we started speaking in a different language. "Well if you really want to know what I think," Lucien says as he pours cereal into his bowl, spilling the contents. "I think that you need to treat her like *cai png*."

Quinn turns to Donny. "Do you know his *cai png* analogy?"

"Yes, I do," Donny says, the corners of his lips twitching. "I was there when Lucy came up with it."

Lucien picks up stray pieces of cereal off the table and place them into his cupped palm. "Caroline is used to people being entertained by her, desperate to continue the conversation at any cost. So on the day that she's met with the right kind of silence, she will be forced to reveal what she is. Lost."

The smirk disappears from Quinn's face. Donny cocks his head towards Lucien, waiting for him to continue. Seemingly oblivious to the effect of his words, Lucien begins to casually eat the pieces of cereal in his palm like a goat in a petting zoo. "Don't you think that life is like unmilked cereal –" he starts.

"We're talking about Caroline, Lucy," Donny says.

Lucien complies. "I think she's still figuring out who she is. She likes fashion but she's not passionate about it. It was more of a natural progression from being a famous influencer. I wasn't there on her first night at The Haven, but I'm guessing her reaction to meeting that famous Korean designer wasn't what Donny hoped for."

Quinn turns to Donny curiously. His small smile validates this. She returns to Lucien, impressed.

"Caroline's in a strange place in her life right now and just wants to belong with something, someone," Lucien concludes, pouring milk into his cereal. "You're lucky to be considered."

Quinn is speechless. Donny affectionately cuffs Lucien on the shoulder before looking up at me. "If things go well, as I'm sure they will, I'd like you to invite Caroline to this weekend's pyjamas themed party at The Haven. It's going to be a riot."

It appears that the discussion has reached its end, so I move to bring my empty plate and mug to the kitchen. But before

I get to leave the table, Donny reaches across and hands me a condom. He laughs loudly at the look on my face. "Break open in case of escalation!"

*

Caroline's afternoon commitments extend into the evening so we change locations to one with a flexible seating schedule. Donny recommends me a tapas bar. He knows the owner, one Rick Ngui, personally, and ensures that the two of us get a private table with the best view of the city.

I feel like a kid going to a prom when I leave The Haven. Donny is eager to send me but he has drinks with clients so Lucien offers to drive me instead. Quinn insists that if I refuse to even put on a blazer over my T-shirt, I should at least let her style my hair again. I agree to it and thank her for her trouble. After she is done, Lucien and I make our move.

The car ride is considerably quieter than it would have been if Donny had driven me. Lucien hums along to the song on the radio as we go down the highway. It is only as we are nearing the bar that Lucien finally speaks. "Can I ask you a question?" he says.

I'd prefer if you didn't, but you were kind enough to drive me here so it is rude for me to say no.

"Yes."

"Are you in love?"

I glance at him. His eyes are focused on the road. When Donny drives he keeps only one hand on the wheel so that the other hand is free to gesticulate, but Lucien has both hands steadfast on the wheel, in full concentration of what's happening in front of him. "I only ask this because you seem hesitant to have dinner with the most beautiful woman in the city. There can only be three possibilities, and I'm just going to strike out the fourth possibility of you not being attracted to her because that is defying gravity."

"Three possibilities?"

"The first one is the bro code. You think that Donny is attracted to Caroline and so you think it's wrong to go out on a date with her. I assure you that his fascination with her is nothing romantic or sexual."

"I wasn't −"

"The second possibility is that you are exactly where you want to be in life. Whether it's because you are not attracted to women that way, or that you don't have the money to maintain her lifestyle, or that you're not comfortable with physical interactions, you simply refuse to step out of your comfort zone. I can completely relate in any case."

"And the third is..."

"The third possibility, which happens to be the most likely one, ties in to the reason why your luggage is still unpacked. You're yearning for something and nothing else will suffice. You're in love."

I don't want to answer him and he knows it. He shrugs his shoulders. "Forgive me. You probably feel like we're ganging up on you. Donny tried to do the same thing for me before, by the way. But I tell you, if you let it be known that you feel uncomfortable with something, he won't force you into it. I think he just likes the feeling of bringing people happiness. He's selfishly altruistic that way."

"So why didn't you do it?"

"I don't care about other people enough to actively −"

"I mean why didn't you let Donny set you up?"

Lucien smiles to himself. "Because I'm in love. I told you that when we went grocery shopping."

"Are the two of you still together?"

"We are when I close my eyes. But that would be unwise

because I'm currently operating machinery."

"You don't want to act on it?"

"No, I do not. I don't think that I could handle the thought of causing her any more grief than I already have. She's been through enough. And now we're here."

"What status is that?"

"No, I mean we've reached the restaurant."

I look up and see the entrance of a hotel with a giant fountain at the entrance and two lion statues on both sides of a flight of marbled steps. There is an outdoor bar next to the drop-off point, where people are drinking cocktails under mellow lights.

"Garamond," he says, pointing to the poster standee outside the bar showing drink promotions. "What a beautiful font."

I want to tell him that it looks like Times New Roman to me but resist the urge for fear of offending him. Lucien parks the car and tilts his head towards me. "Go into the lobby, turn right to reach the elevators and head up to the 20th floor. The table's reserved under your name."

I thank him for the ride and step out of the car. He says to me, "Let's have a proper conversation someday."

"I'd like that."

I mean it, too.

He smiles. "Have a good night. Let me know if you need a ride back. I'll be working on a couple of projects till late."

I do not shut the door immediately and Lucien laughs. "Ha ha ha. Relax. The two of you are going to have a great time. Even if you're at a loss for words, it's in Caroline's nature to help you find them. She's going to do everything in her bag of tricks to make you comfortable because you look like someone familiar to her. In fact, from some angles it is uncanny."

"Who do I look like?"

Lucien beams at me. "Like someone at the top of the food chain."

*

When I arrive, Rick is already at the main entrance waiting for me. He shakes my hand cheerily as though we have known each other for years. He guides me through the restaurant past tables of couples chatting over candlelight to the rooftop. It has a seating capacity of over ten tables under fairy lights but the area is completely empty. He leads me to a table at the edge of the bar that overlooks the entire Singapore nightscape.

"Our mutual friend tells me that this is a very special date. He booked out the entire roof for the two of you."

Overkill, thy name is Donny.

"That was not necessary."

"Nonsense. This is nothing compared to what Donny has done for me over the years. Please stay as long as you want and order as much as you like."

I take my seat and order a gin and tonic to calm my nerves. Every so often I glance over at the entrance but my worries are premature. It is almost half an hour later when Caroline shows up, walking through the crowd as though under a follow light. I watch her make her way to me as the entire restaurant goes quiet, watching her pass. She is positively glowing.

When Caroline joins me at the rooftop, she leans in to kiss me on the cheek before taking the seat next to me. I feel our knees graze against each other as she sits down.

"What a beautiful place," Caroline says, looking around the bar area and the night view. "Did you book out the entire area for us?"

"Donny did."

"What showmanship. I guess he wanted you to impress me. Was he the one who recommended this place?"

"Yes he was."

"Ah. I presumed that it was Zephyr."

I flinch at the casual mention of the name but say nothing. Rick makes his way over and begins recommending dishes. He is very complimentary towards the two of us, laughing at everything Caroline says and telling her how handsome I am and how lucky she is. His charm is cringe worthy at times, but Caroline's reactions make him seem spellbinding.

After Caroline orders a bottle of red wine and several tapas, Rick rubs me on the shoulder in a strangely fatherly manner and walks off. She smiles at me when we are alone again.

"I have a confession to make. Would you like to hear it?"

"Yes."

"I was wondering when you'd finally ask me out."

"I bet you're not used to that."

"What?"

"Hesitation."

Her look in answer is more than attractive. It is a well-practised cheekiness.

Rick returns with a bottle of red wine and two glasses. After he is done with the routine of asking her to taste and setting the cork down, he pours the wine. She nods and expects him to leave but he boldly asks if she would be so kind as to post about his restaurant on Instagram.

"I'm sorry, I don't do that anymore," she says apologetically.

"We can pay. I can do it on top of the free dinner and drinks, it's no problem."

"I appreciate that, but I don't post on Instagram anymore."

"You're *morethanfourleafclover* right? My daughter watches

your Wednesday videos religiously. She loves helping you decide what to wear and eat."

"I used to do that, but not anymore. I'd be happy to send a personal video to your daughter if you'd like, though. It'd be my honour."

Disappointed, Rick thanks her and leaves with a dejected look on his face.

"That must happen quite a bit," I say.

"More than you think. I guess I'm not the easiest person in the world to date." Then she looks thoughtful as if counting silently to herself. "It's been a while since I've been on one, actually."

"I'm honoured."

"So is that what this is?"

"What do you mean?"

"You're saying that this is a date?"

She picks up her wine glass and holds it up towards me. We touch glasses and she takes a sip with a happy hum.

"Why don't you post on Instagram anymore?" I ask her.

Caroline's smile fades slightly before it lights up her face again. "It's a little too early in the night to talk about such heavy matters. Ask me again when we finish this bottle."

I do not press the issue. She sets her glass down on the table. "I'm sure that Madam Mischief and the others have told you a lot about me. I want to know more about you. Let's make a game out of it. I'll ask you a personal question, and you ask me one in return. And we keep this up until we become properly acquainted."

I want to tell her that there really isn't that much to know about me. She takes my continued silence as consent.

"If I'm getting too personal, do let me know and I'll stop. I have the habit of being too inquisitive."

I nod. It seems like there is nothing else I can do.

I have been on first dates before. The first half an hour is usually an awkward affair of sussing each other out before the decision is made whether attraction is evident or if the evening will maintain its awkwardness. I ready myself for her to ask about my family or friends or favourite colour but her line of inquisition surprises me.

"If you could turn into any animal, what would you want to become?"

What?

"What?"

"If you could turn into any animal you want," she repeats. "What animal would you want to be?"

She watches me furtively till I'm forced to answer.

"A killer whale? Perhaps."

"Why?"

"Because it's playful yet sensitive. It's brave and protective, and it's the only animal that can take down a shark."

She looks satisfied with my answer, inclining her head in my direction as a cue for me to ask her something in return. I think about it for a moment. "If you had to describe yourself as a food item, what would you be?" I ask.

She laughs loudly, clapping her hands together as she does so. "Yay, you went with the strange! I like that. I'm a banana split. I'm hot and cold, a tad nutty, flexible with flavours and I'll drive you bananas."

That was quick-witted, almost practiced.

"My turn," she says, rubbing her hands together with glee. Then she pulls out her cigarettes, holding one up as though asking for permission. I nod and she proceeds to light up. "Have you ever been in a fight before?"

I nod my head and her mouth forms into an "o". She eggs me on to tell her. It was with Zephyr, because of Zephyr.

"It's a long story," I say.

"Perfect. I've got the whole night."

So I tell her.

*

It started on the night when I noticed a scratch on Zephyr's chin. She was moodily smoking a cigarette on our park bench. She forced a smile as I approached. I asked her where the scratch came from and she flippantly told me that it was self-inflicted. Always able to tell when she was lying, I persisted and she eventually told me the truth.

Her older brother's girlfriend had cheated on him. He had suspicions and had trailed the two to a love hotel and confronted them when they exited two hours later. While waiting, he had called Zephyr and said he would beat them up and kill him. Zephyr rushed to the hotel and found her brother in a heated altercation with his girlfriend and her lover. Zephyr stepped in and used some not-so-friendly words on the woman who slapped her and inflicted the scratch.

Zephyr was mid-way into the story when she received a phone call from her brother's number.

She answered the call, only to hear an abrasive voice spewing expletives at her. It was her brother's girlfriend. Zephyr's brother had gone to confront them once again and Zephyr was dragged into the argument.

The girl had called to challenge Zephyr to a fight.

What a bizarre turn of events. Without a moment's hesitation, Zephyr rose to her feet.

"I'm sorry but I need to settle this. I'll see you another time."

I stood up, taking her by surprise. "I'm coming with you," I said.

"Can you fight?" She looked at me like she wanted to laugh.

"Yes, I can."

"You just swallowed. You should try to lie a little more convincingly."

"You need backup."

"Then guard our palace while I'm gone. I'll settle this and meet you back here."

I told her that she was being ludicrous. I insisted on following her.

"I don't know how this will pan out, electric eel."

"I'm not going to change my mind."

"It's —"

"I'm going with you. End of discussion."

She was reluctant but I flagged us a taxi and we hopped in. During the entire ride Zephyr was silent. I reached over and held her hand. She clasped mine tightly.

We arrived at the appointed HDB void deck. Zephyr's brother was sitting at a table with his girlfriend and her new man. Behind them were ten scowling hooligans.

"You Zapper ah?" one of them said, pointing as we approached.

"Yes, I am," she replied.

He walked forward and reached out to shake Zephyr's hand. This action looked akin to a punch. Unflinchingly, she reached out and shook it.

"I'm Yong Kee. You call me Kee can already," he said. "We here only to be referee. I promise that I will not touch you. Same for my boys."

"That's kind of you. I'd like you to do the same for my friend."

He looked at me. I tried my best to look as unthreatening as possible, which was not difficult. He nodded. "Okay. Promise."

"Thank you."

"Look at the scratch on her face. That was me!" the girl

yelled in triumph. She was tiny. She didn't even come to Zephyr's shoulders.

"What would you like to do?" Zephyr asked, ignoring her.

"Fight la," Kee said with a toss of his head. "She wants one-to-one with you. So you fight then okay *liao*. We won't interfere."

I almost laughed but he was deadly serious. The girl pointed at Zephyr. "You tell the bitch that she can pick location. Don't anyhow say I homeground advantage all."

Kee said to Zephyr that she had three choices: the toilet, the elevator and the car park. I hid my bewilderment as he explained the terms. For the toilet, the two girls would be locked in one of the cubicles. One member of the gang would be in each of the other cubicles, flushing them one after another. The two women would fight for as long as it took for all the toilet bowls to flush. The elevator option would start with them on level 28, the top floor, fighting till they reached the ground floor. And for the car park, it would be on the slope of the top floor where they would fight for as long as it took Kee to smoke a cigarette.

Zephyr weighed her options.

"Car park," she said, to the loud hoots of the guys.

Later, she told me the reason for her choice. Her biggest concern was that the girl potentially concealed a weapon. The lift and toilet would make it difficult for her to dodge or escape.

So we went to the top level of the car park, where half the guys waited below the slope and the others stood at the top. I was still in denial of a fight happening until I saw the girl limbering up in a corner.

Zephyr's brother and I stood with Zephyr anxiously. "What are you going to do?" her brother asked. His face was ghastly white. "I didn't know that you knew how to fight."

"I don't," she said.

"Then what are you going to do?" I asked as Zephyr's brother's eyes bulged almost comically.

She shrugged. "I'm going to beat the shit out of this garden gnome and then we're going home."

The car park was completely empty. Zephyr and the girl squared up. Kee stood aside, an unlit cigarette hanging from his lips. All eyes were on him as he took his time to pull out his lighter dramatically.

"Ready?" he said.

Zephyr shrugged. If she was hiding her fear she was doing it incredibly well. The other girl nodded, looking ready to inflict pain on my best friend. Kee lit his cigarette. The girl, screaming at the top of her lungs, dashed towards Zephyr and tackled her down. She grabbed Zephyr's hair and looked like slamming her head on the ground.

I made a motion to dash forward but one of the guys grabbed my arm. "Don't like that, bro," he said. "Don't make us whack you. This is your first and last warning ah."

Zephyr must have taken three hits in a row to the back of her head. Then she snapped to action and grabbed the girl by the neck and flipped her around till she was on top of her. The gangsters were incredibly restrained. None of them said a word. In a wild fury, Zephyr began scratching at the girl's face with everything she had. She was an agile, beautiful feline. The girl was screaming, trying to cover her face but Zephyr pushed her knee into the girl's diaphragm, making her gasp for breath as she continued her assault on the girl's face.

I glanced at Kee. He was not even halfway into his cigarette. He caught my eye and shrugged. The girl began to scream for help. Zephyr was not stopping. Something had taken over her and it was thrilling to watch. The girl was beginning to cry. You could hear it in her voice. She continued to scream for help but none of her friends budged. Suddenly the home wrecker rushed forward.

Till this day I do not know what possessed me, but I dashed forward too, flailing wildly at him. I aimed a punch at his jaw but missed and hit him in the forehead. I felt my hand ache as his eyes flashed, turning his attention to me and began swinging haymakers.

He could clearly fight. Every single one of his punches connected. I crumbled to my feet uselessly, and he burst at me for the final blow before Zephyr stepped in front of me. Before he had a chance to exercise his anger on her, the other guys had stepped in to stop the fight from escalating. The strong, sullen look on Zephyr's face was powerful beyond words.

"Stop," she said simply in cold fury. "Or I'll make your face unrecognisable."

Zephyr had won the fight fair and square.

We were back at the park bench. Zephyr got two bags of peas from her freezer and we used them on our heads. My jaw felt swollen.

"I'm sorry, electric eel. I didn't want you to see me like that," she said.

"You looked bold and beautiful. Don't ever apologise for that."

She grinned at me. "I looked beautiful?"

"You did. You do. You always do."

She pulled on her cigarette and let out a deep breath. Then she turned to me with a wry grin. "Kehehe. I told you that I would beat the shit out of her."

"Technically you scratched the hell out of her."

"Oh, whatever."

*

Caroline is immersed throughout the story. She gasps at moments and almost applauds when I describe Zephyr clawing at the girl's face.

"What an experience. You and Zephyr have a beautiful friendship," she says.

Yes, we do. Thank you.

"Why does she call you electric eel?"

I blink, taken aback by her question. Caroline smiles.

"During your story you mentioned that she calls you electric eel."

A part of me does not want to tell her. It feels too close to home. Zephyr came up with the nickname from a quote by one of her favourite poets, Edith Sitwell. It goes along the lines of, "I'm not eccentric. It's that I'm more alive than most. I am an unpopular electric eel set in a pond of catfish."

It is her way of telling me that I am strange and special. It is more than just a nickname; it is a reminder. Every time Zephyr calls me this, she does it with an unflinching gaze, making sure I am the only person in her line of vision. As undeserving as I am of the name, it makes me smile every time I hear it.

"It appears that I crossed the line," Caroline says before I say anything. She smiles apologetically. "Forget I asked."

"No, don't worry about it."

Rick interrupts us. He's back to accept Caroline's offer to make a video specially for his daughter. He hands Caroline his phone with both hands and tells her that his daughter's name is Emily.

Caroline takes the phone and presses the video record button.

"Hello Emily!" she coos. "Here's a big, giant thank you for

supporting me all this while. I want to tell you to please do well in school and listen to your parents and teachers but I'm sure you're a smart cookie, so I'll just say embrace and celebrate all that you can in this funny little world."

The things that Caroline does with her voice is amazing: modulations and stretching vowels turn common words into something meaningful and captivating. She finishes. Rick takes his phone from her, bowing gratefully, leaving us alone again.

"Sorry about that," she says.

"It's no problem at all. I'm impressed that you did that in one take."

"No, not the video," she says sheepishly. "The voice. I'm used to putting on this tone for the camera because back when I was still active on social media, it gave me the highest engagement."

"Oh. No, it's fine. You have a very nice voice."

"On camera or off camera?"

"Both, really."

"But which do you prefer?"

"I like your voice right now."

She beams. "I'll keep that in mind. It's for you. Exclusively."

Wow, Caroline, you are ridiculously smooth.

The food arrives and we eat. The table is rich with the colour and flavour of Spanish omelette, sautéed cauliflower with pine nuts and onion, steamed mussels, pork ribs in pumpkin puree, grilled scallops and the restaurant's signature squid ink paella.

Caroline takes a sip of her wine. She pauses, looks at me thoughtfully and asks, "Do you have to head back to The Haven after this?"

Without waiting for my answer, she continues, "I'd like to bring you somewhere after we're done here."

"Where?"

She beams at me from across the table. "You'll see."

*

Caroline has a beautiful apartment. Taking my hand, she guides me to the balcony where there are two red lounge chairs. It feels like we are hovering over the edge of the world. Caroline sits, her legs pulled close, hugging her knees. The wind is blowing in her hair, shadows cascading on her face in the midnight glow. She turns to me with a smile.

"Are you enjoying yourself?" she asks.

"Absotively. I-I mean yes," I say. My words are beginning to slur as I sink deeper and deeper into the lounge chair. I have had more than three drinks tonight. This is not a good thing. I should make my move soon.

Caroline laughs. "So anyway, I know that Donny nearly had to tie you up to get you to me tonight."

"It's nothing personal. I'm just horrible with social interactions."

She leans in and I catch a whiff of her scent. It is a curious cocktail of perfume, wine and cigarettes. "I love the personal. And I think you're doing just fine. I'm glad you asked me out."

Her voice, as always, ensnares. I know that is her intended effect. "So you wanted to know me better," I say.

Caroline tosses her hair back and laughs. "If you have to summarise unromantically, yes. Throughout the night I have been sneaking glances at you to see if I've managed to make you smile or laugh. I guess I want to impress you. I couldn't say this until I was sure your liquid courage kicked in."

"Donny does that."

Caroline smiles mirthlessly. "Donny's such a sharp guy. He knew that I'd be attracted to you, you know. Quinn warned me not to let him get inside my head but as soon as we met he could see all these nuances that I thought I hid so well. When you display your entire life for the public to see, nobody bothers to look closer. Nobody except Donny."

"What did he see?"

Something foreign crosses Caroline's face. It is only for an instant but I recognise it.

"Melancholy," she says, drawing a cigarette to her lips, lighting it and exhaling a whiff of smoke. "Isn't that such a beautiful word?"

"Melancholy?"

"Yes, melancholy. It sounds like a French dessert. It sounds like a musical instrument with strings and a hollow frame. It sounds like a city surrounded by forest and rain."

"It sounds like a flower that glows in your hands," I say.

She looks at me with a fixed gaze, face flushed and eyes wide. Then she smiles softly. "Yeah, exactly," she says.

Caroline removes her phone case and takes out a worn-out photograph from inside it. It is a photo of her kissing the cheek of a man. She looks much younger then, her hair is dyed light brown and she has coloured contact lenses on. The young man next to her has short hair like an NS man. He looks a bit like me.

She laughs mirthlessly. "What a cliché, huh? No one keeps Polaroids anymore, everything is up on Instagram."

"That's not true. I think that a Polaroid shows significance."

Caroline smiles. She begins to tell me about him. Her boyfriend's name was Michael. Michael Hou. She called him Houdini because she thought that he was magic. He was quiet and reserved but he had a brilliant mind. He would go quiet for long bouts of the day and then out of the blue he would say something so potent and sincere that it would leave her breathless. The two of them did everything together. He was a photographer and helped her with her online content. He helped her scout for photoshoot locations and took her OOTDs and product shots. Her popular #DecideForMeWednesdays, which skyrocketed her fame, was his idea.

Not once did he complain when she was stopped on the street for photos with fans or had to wait for hours till she was done with meetings and events. They savoured every moment together, even though there was almost always a camera in between them. Caroline's fans would know where they went for anniversary dinners, what he got her for her birthdays, how his first meeting with her parents went, as well as the details of adventures that the two of them shared. Sometimes, strangers would know about the depths of their relationship even before he did. Such as her insecurities regarding his being with other women, her stance on abortion, or how lonely she felt when he travelled for work. She would pour her heart out to her fans and they provided her with advice, comfort and love.

She had everything locked down for the two of them. From her rise to fame when she was getting sponsorships from younger demographic fashion brands, to fashion products and big makeup brands when her career was established. There were sponsors lined up and waiting for their eventual marriage – flowers, venues, photographers and videographers, to a cake, food and drinks, her gowns and his suits, all the way down to wedding favours.

Then one day, everything crashed. Half a year ago, Michael and his photographer friends decided to take a trip up to Mount Everest Base Camp. He never came back. Something went wrong. She could not contact him for days. She broke down the moment his best friend showed up at her door with Michael's camera.

At this moment of her story, Caroline's voice breaks as she buries her face in her hands.

"Do you know what's messed up? The first thing that crossed my mind was to find somewhere quiet to go on Instagram Live. But when I switched it on, I could not muster up the courage to do anything. I found myself suddenly speechless. Users joined my live video within seconds. The viewers rose and continued rising. People began to comment on my hair, my makeup, my outfit, showering me with greetings and compliments. Then someone mentioned Houdini's name and I snapped. I smiled. I smiled like the world was mine. I began talking about myself. I told my audience about the next event that I'd be at, I promoted one of the brands that I was being endorsed by, I shared about what I'd be eating that evening, how excited I was and how amazing a time I was having when I realised mid-way through that the most honest person in Singapore was a fraud."

"Don't say that."

She shakes her head. "That was the last time I posted on my feed. I can't even go on my profile without thinking of him. I remember his smile behind the camera every time he took a photo of me. I remember how he looked at me adoringly every time he captured me in the light that he wanted. Every good photo I have on *morethanfourleafclover* is his. My job feels joyless now. I don't believe in magic anymore and I just wish that I had somehow forced him not to go..."

The cigarette slips from her fingers and falls to the balcony floor. I pick it up and stub it out in the ashtray. We are quiet for some time. Then she eventually emerges from her hands and is smiling brightly, dried tears and streaked mascara on her face. It is painful to witness. She wipes the stains away. She returns the photograph to her phone case. We stay in silence.

"Can I ask you a question?" she asks, finally.

"Ask me anything," I say. I mean it too.

"What made you decide to become a social media manager?"

"It was not a decision; I was chosen. It is all I ever want to be in life."

"Really?"

"No. I'm sorry, that was a bad attempt at a joke."

"Oh!" Caroline says, smiling weakly. "Sorry. I wasn't expecting that."

"My ex-girlfriend wanted to create a marketing agency and needed my help. It was the side of business that did not require dealing with clients."

She laughs. It is a welcoming sound from her. "You really hate socialising."

"I became good at social media management without having any passion for it whatsoever. Our first client was my roommate. She was selling her flower arrangements and needed someone to run her Instagram. We sold a lot of flowers, and she moved out in six months because she could afford an apartment of her own. So I moved back in with my mother."

"Flowers are a great business to be in. Why did you say ex?"

"I did? I guess they were. About $90 per bouquet, give or take."

"I meant ex-girlfriend."

"Oh."

"You don't have to tell me if you don't want to – "

"When we started to expand we began hiring. We had about 10 people in our team when we lost four clients in a month. Unwilling to downsize, Andrea – "

"That's your ex-girlfriend's name?"

"Yeah, her name is Andrea. So we needed an investor. There

was this client who had taken a keen interest to her. He would come down to the office for the strangest of reasons. When he found out about our difficulties, he agreed to invest."

"I see where this is going," Caroline says, wrinkling her nose.

"You're correct. One night I went down to the office to get some work done and found them together."

"That's awful."

"So things got a little awkward after that, and a couple of weeks later, I was called into the conference room and was let go."

Caroline covers her mouth with her hands.

"Then I bumped into Donny and he told me about The Haven and now I'm here. That's my story."

Her fingers slowly drop from her face to expose a smile. "And now you're here," she says. "I must say I'm happy that you've loosened your lips."

"It's because of the alcohol. I try to limit myself to three drinks."

"Why would you do something like that?"

"I don't like being out of control, sloshed and stirred. I sound silly."

Caroline shakes her head. "No, Melbourne boy. I like that you've opened up. You sound like magic."

I cannot imagine how one voice box can have so many cadences and tonal shifts as seamless as jazz.

"Your Instagram handle. Why do you call yourself *morethanfourleafclover*?"

She pauses for a moment, putting down her cigarettes and turns to me. "Ah, that. Mister social media expert, what would you think?"

"Four leaf clovers are for good luck, so I'm presuming that's what you're alluding to?"

"Fair. A lot of people think that. But it's because of my birthmark."

"Your birthmark?"

"Mmhmm."

She leans ever so slightly forward and points to her right breast.

"It's here. You need to be close to see it."

When I make no motion forward, she hooks a finger on the neckline of her dress and lowers it, presumably to show me her concealed birthmark. I avert my gaze and unintentionally recoil. Caroline notices this and looks surprised, and a little hurt.

"Ah," she says, laughing but there is a hint of sourness that does not go unhidden. "I see."

"It's not what I –"

"You don't have to explain. I understand. Sorry if I made you uncomfortable."

She wraps her knees close to her chest again and looks up at the sky. There is a sad smile playing on her lips.

"You must think I'm broken."

We have asked each other many questions tonight but this is the only one that matters. She has poured her heart out. It seems only fair that I respect her by being honest in return.

"I think that you're someone who fought her heart out to get here," I say. She turns to meet my gaze. "I don't know the scene here well, but I can tell that you're one of the lucky few in the centre of it. I also think your attraction to me is misguided. I just remind you of someone who you once loved – you love."

Something is dawning on her. It's quiet, subtle, but potent.

"You need an equal," I continue. "And he isn't me. Don't settle just because you feel lost. You deserve much more than that. And I want more than that too."

She looks like she is about to cry again but then her face breaks into a watery smile. "Now that was magic," she says softly. She reaches down to her pack of cigarettes, takes one stick out, lights it and blows out a thin stream of smoke.

"And you? Are you in love with someone?" she asks.

It's complicated.

"Is it Zephyr?"

"Yes it is," I hear myself saying.

"Do you want to be with her right now?"

"Yes, I do."

Her eyes stay on me as she tilts her head towards the door, unflinching and unbroken. "Then what are you waiting for?" she says.

The silence after that extends till it turns literal, stretching further and further till I am in the elevator of her apartment block, down to the lobby, inside a taxi and off into the night.

*

I'm back at the park bench. Zephyr is there with a cigarette between her fingers. She smiles as I approach. "Hey there, stranger."

"Hey. How's the castle?"

"Exactly how you left it. How was your date?"

"It's midnight and I'm here."

I take a seat next to her. She rests her head on my shoulder. Looking down at the ground, from the way our shadows are touching, it looks like we have both leaned in to lock lips. I ask her about her day and she tells me that her agency is having problems. They are having a tough month and one of their biggest clients might be poached by a larger outfit.

"Donny is throwing another party at The Haven," I tell her. "You might meet some potential leads there. Would you come? I would love it if you were there."

Zephyr smiles, stubbing out her cigarette and tossing it into the empty can of Pringles next to her.

"I would love to, electric eel."

I feel like my heart is about to burst as I lean my head against Zephyr's. She is humming happily under her breath. I glance down at her. Her eyes are shut.

"I'd like to tell you about Andrea," I say to her.

Eyes still closed, she nods. "Your mother told me that I'm prettier than her."

"Oh, are you now?"

"Your mother's words, not mine," she says. She smiles to herself. "Tell me about her, Will."

When I am finished, we do not say a word for a long time. Zephyr's head on my shoulder is beginning to make my collarbone ache. I look down and realise that she has fallen asleep. She gives a small shiver against me and I smile to myself. Here I am, entrusted with her good dream to keep it safe. I make it my duty to keep it safe.

"Safe here, eel," she mumbles. She is talking in her sleep.

I kiss the top of her forehead.

"Yes I am, Zeph," I say.

"Oh my God, you're a douche."

When I wake up the next morning, Lucien is cooking *nasi lemak* for guests in the kitchen. There is a mountain of rice, a huge bowl of sambal and plates of chopped up cucumbers, fried eggs, *sotong* balls and *ikan bilis* on the table. He is deep-frying chicken cutlets when he sees me and beams brightly.

"Good morning!" he says. "Fancy some breakfast?"

Donny is leaning forward in his seat at the kitchen island, his attention focused on one of the guests. I recognise him to be the male model Isaac. He has a jaunty grin on his face but his eyes remain cold as always. With him are three beautiful young women dressed in floral dresses of different colours. One of them barks an order to Lucien, making a joke about his clothing but he does not bat an eyelid.

"My beauty is on the inside, Clarissa," he says lightly. "Not everyone gets to light up the world like you do. Now who was the one who wanted scrambled eggs instead of fried eggs?"

"That would be me," Clarissa says. "I told you just a few minutes ago. What kind of second rate service is this?"

"I beg your pardon," he says, putting a pan on the stove and walking to the refrigerator to get more eggs.

I sit down at the far end of the kitchen island away from the ladies, where Donny and Isaac are in conversation.

"Thanks for having us over for breakfast, Donny," Isaac says. "I wanted to introduce you to a few friends of mine."

"You're always welcome to The Haven," Donny says. He pats me on the shoulder. "Hello Romeo, slept well? I'm surprised that you ended up in your own bed last night."

Isaac tilts his head at me. "Did someone have a date last night?"

"Yes, he did."

"Who with? Is she hot?"

"You're not going to like the answer."

Isaac falters as he glares at me. "You better say that it's my sister because if it's Caroline, I swear – "

"All this angst in the morning is unhealthy for the soul," Donny says, nodding gratefully as Lucien walks over with the frying pan and tips a chicken cutlet onto his plate. "She came over for one of my parties and took a fancy towards my friend. I can't blame her for having good taste."

Isaac snorts. "So she made the first move, eh? What a slut."

"Would you like me to do the sour grapes routine again, Isaac?"

Isaac reclines in his chair haughtily. "So how was she?" he says to me. "Was she an easy bitch to lay?"

"Don't call her that," I say.

Donny raises his eyebrows at me. Isaac's face falls and he sits upright. "Oh my God, you fell for the siren song," he says, edging away from me as though I am carrying something infectious. "Trust me bro, you don't know her."

"And you know her?"

I don't think my tone has any malice in it. It is just a simple question. But Donny is looking at me as though I have just swung a punch at Isaac. He looks amused too.

Isaac replies with a toothy sneer. "Wow, all you need now is a mask and a cape. I'm trying to help you dude. I have a lot of women. I know a slut when I see one. I can also tell that she's got an ego."

"That's a bit rich coming from you, Isaac," Donny says. "Your phone wallpaper is a picture of yourself bare-chested on a sailboat."

Donny says this with a squint, daring Isaac to retort. He looks sorely tempted to do so but Isaac conceals his irritation, albeit poorly, by laughing a little too loudly. "Hey man, I'm just trying to impart wisdom," he says to his host while patting me on the shoulder. He means to make this come across as good-natured, but it just feels like he's cleaning his dirty hand on my shirt.

Donny begins to dig into his breakfast with a smile on his face. "If you're looking for the perfect moment to ask me for a favour, now's as good a time as any," he says. "Don't waste that elegant surrender."

Isaac whistles. "How'd you know I need a favour?"

"You've been glancing around, you tensed up the moment my friend joined us and we're three seats away from the others. Obviously there's something private you'd like to discuss."

"This is why you're so successful in expanding your family's chilli sauce empire," Isaac says, attempting to flatter Donny. "Nothing slips past your gaze."

Donny ignores him and turns his attention to the shrieking laughter coming from the girls' corner. They have not stopped teasing Lucien, even as he places chicken cutlets on their plates.

"You're a great cook!" one of the girls say. "This is super yummy."

Lucien bows flamboyantly.

"But with the way you dress, you're never going to get a girl. Big deal if you can cook like a Masterchef," Clarissa says.

"Are you gay?"

"No, I'm not."

"There's no need to be shy, if you're gay just say so, I won't judge."

"I have to admit, with your promise of no judgment, all my fears in the universe are dispersed," Lucien says. "But I'm not."

"Then have you had a girlfriend before?"

"Yes, I have."

"I'll bet she's blind or has no taste," Clarissa says, and the other girls burst out laughing. The placid smile on Lucien's face freezes.

Donny glances over at Isaac who is mulling up a storm. "Are those close friends of yours?" he says.

"Not particularly, but there's a reason why I invited them here, my clever friend," Isaac begins his foreshadowing. "Do you fancy any of them?"

"They're being rude to Lucy. I'd like you to tell them to stop."

"Oh, come on, they're just teasing. Lucien is just your housemate, right?"

"No, he's my friend."

"Tell me what her name is," Clarissa insists. "I want to find her on Facebook."

"I would not like that," Lucien says.

"Why not! Is she ugly?"

"No, she's beautiful."

"Then stop being so secretive! C'mon, I want to see her."

"I am uncomfortable about giving her personal details merely to satisfy your curiosity. Let's leave it at that. Does anyone want more food?"

"Oh, stop being such a wet blanket. You're pretty much admitting that she's ugly. If she's as hot as you claim, you'd surely show us her photo. Don't make me go up to your room right now, I'll bet there's a picture of her in there for your – "

"Clarissa."

Donny says her name in a tone unlike his own, and the laughter dissipates immediately as she turns to him like a schoolgirl being called out in front of the class by a teacher. She meets his stern look from across the table. His message is given without another word. Then he smiles at her, the cold fury disappearing without a trace.

"Could you pass the sambal? It's delicious, isn't it?"

She nods numbly, handing the bowl to him. "Yes, Louscy is a great cook."

"His name is Lucien," he corrects her.

"Lu-ci-en, sorry."

Donny is still smiling, but the ladies fall silent. He turns back to Isaac. "I'm sorry, you were saying?"

Isaac is taken aback. That display of power from Donny appears to further compound his convictions. He reaches into his pocket and pulls out a name card. Donny looks at it, his expression unchanging. I can see Donny's name on it. He flips the card over and there is a logo of a woman's silhouette and the name "The Paradise". Donny meets Isaac's gaze curiously.

"You have my attention."

"I figured as much. It took me a while, but The Paradise is now officially in business. I created an elevated experience where men can enjoy pleasure without feeling sleazy. From the moment they enter the doors, the guests are treated like royalty. No photography is allowed for privacy's sake, the welcome drink is whiskey in a personalised engraved glass, a host is always present to fulfil every need and desire, and as the logo states, there is a wide selection of beautiful women for the picking."

Donny glances at the women now well behaved and polite as Lucien busies himself with making a fresh pot of coffee.

"So, these 'friends' of yours are part of the catalogue?" Donny says with appropriate emphasis.

"They're my most popular girls. Looking at them, I'm sure you understand why."

"If I denied the dimensions, sure."

"There will be three tiers of women based on experience, beauty and even aggression. Many of them are models. I've got girls from Korea, Taiwan, Hong Kong, China, Thailand, Vietnam, America, the Middle East and of course, locals. Every preference of our male guests will be catered to," Isaac says, gesturing to the women. "After you pick your girl, you get to choose what outfit they wear. Anything you want. Am I right, ladies?"

"Yes!" they reply in unison.

"We offer freelancers comfortable with their bodies and happy to earn a pretty penny for it. This isn't a mirage. It's a modern oasis. It's paradise."

"That was well-practised," Donny says. "You seem to have thought this through. What do you need me for?"

There is an edge of anger in his tone but Isaac, too engrossed in his own brilliance, fails to notice it.

"I'm a backend guy, no pun intended."

"Liar."

"I'm not great with customer relations. People find me too intimidating. That's why I need a man of your specific talents. What you do for your dad's business is incredible. I've seen you at work. I've seen you notice a girl's new hairstyle even if she cuts it a centimetre shorter. I see you realise people's hidden wants and desires before even meeting them. I see people opening up to you like they're automatic doors. I could use someone brilliant like you. We'd be perfect together."

"That's still not an answer."

"I want to tap into The Haven's database. You have wealthy men coming in and out of your establishment every night, and beautiful women who love having a good time. There's our synergy. With the way you are, able to spot what people are comfortable with from the get-go, we can do this seamlessly. I'm more than happy to give you a healthy commission. I know that you don't need the money, but – "

"You're right."

"Huh?"

"I don't need the money."

Donny sits before Isaac, fingers knitted on his lap, staring at him calmly. Amazingly, Isaac is oblivious of the body language.

"Look, why don't you just visit The Paradise before you make your decision?" Isaac says. "You can bring your housemates along. Drinks and girls will be on the house. At the very least give me some advice on how to improve my establishment. I could really use your help."

"Oh, Quinn would love that," Lucien says, peering at the name card in Donny's hand as he comes over to refill our coffee cups. "Oho, hello there Myriad. You're hiding mayhem behind incredibly versatile letters. Was that intentional? Because if so – brilliant."

Isaac is bewildered.

Donny relaxes. "How about this, Supernova Casanova," he says. "I'll visit your establishment if you come to my party this weekend. I'll show you my specific brand of entertainment."

I turn to Lucien but he does not look the least bit shocked. It appears that Donny's compulsion to help has superseded his revulsion.

Isaac is triumphant. "That's a deal, chilli sauce prince," he says in an effort to be charming but Donny's lips curl.

"I won't take those Paradise name cards, thank you," Donny says. "I'm only going to give you my feedback."

Isaac winks. "Understood. When would you like to come?" stressing the last word crudely.

*

Lucien gets a call for a last-minute lunch meeting. Big Baller Brandon apparently had a Big Brilliant Brainwave and demanded that Lucien meet him right away. So with a sigh and a quick change of clothes, Lucien heads out of the door. I follow suit soon after.

Whenever Lucien is not at home we tend to get takeout food. None of us enjoy cooking like he does. I am finished buying duck rice for Quinn, Donny and myself from the store across the street when I see a middle-aged man standing outside The Haven. He has round spectacles, wears a grey-collared shirt with black pants and brown covered shoes. He's practically bald. He shuffles his feet nervously and jumps slightly when I approach.

"Oh, hello," he says timidly. His voice is hoarse and croaky.

"May I help you?"

He pushes his glasses up the bridge of his nose but it droops back down. His wipes the beads of sweat from his forehead and asks, "Uh, do you live here?"

"Yes, for the time being."

"Oh, so you're not the owner?"

"No, I'm not. May I help you?"

"Yes.... I mean, no.... It's fine...."

The man takes hurried steps away from me then, stopping in his tracks, turns back. "Do you know the owner?"

"Yes, I do."

"Is he a good person?"

"Yes. He tries more than most people. Are you looking for him?"

"I'm looking for his girlfriend, actually. Or maybe she's just one of his.... I don't know. I don't know what I'm asking. I'm just wondering how she's doing and if she's okay."

"I'm sorry, I don't understand. Who are you looking for?"

"I just want to see if my daughter is safe. Her name is Quinn. Quinn Ong. Do you know who she is?"

"Yes, I know her. In fact, she's inside the house right now. Let me get her."

His bottom lip trembles. He follows me gingerly as I walk towards the gate. Then he stops and bows his head sheepishly.

"Perhaps now's not the right time. I'm sorry for the trouble... please make sure she's alright," he says, and hurries off.

Bewildered, I enter The Haven and look for Donny and Quinn. I tell them about my encounter and Quinn turns pale.

"Did he say anything?" she says quietly.

"He just wanted to know how you are. He's worried. He seemed to think that you are Donny's girlfriend."

She suddenly snorts with laughter. "Yes, it'd be a relief if his daughter was part of a harem rather than a lesbian, wouldn't it?"

"Paradise isn't what I'd call a place like this."

When night falls, we make our way down to The Paradise. By "we" I mean all the inhabitants of The Haven. Donny drives one of his more inconspicuous cars, a black Maserati, nodding his head to the music almost the entire journey like a bobblehead doll.

Isaac's establishment is a two-storey, creamy-white bungalow with black windows shrouded by greenery on top of a hill. A large pool, lit-up in pink neon, is in the front. As soon as we enter the gate, a cheery-looking valet bows, opens the car door for Donny and welcomes us. He takes the car keys and speeds off to the car park.

We walk to the entrance, where two burly-looking men block our way. Their expressions change when Donny tells them who he is. Wide smiles now replace their scowls as they gesture expansively with their arms.

"This isn't a mirage," one says.

"It's a modern oasis," rejoins the other.

"It's paradise," they chorus in unison and bow deeply.

We walk in and the giant doors shut behind us.

"There are already four things that I want to improve about this place," Donny says.

"Will your criticisms make Isaac cry?" Quinn smirks.

"No, my criticisms will make him better," Donny says. "That's the point of us being here."

"To polish up the perversion?" Lucien asks, laughing to himself.

We are now in The Paradise's lobby. It is a cavernous, dimly lit space clad in black marble. A circle of standing chandeliers with smoky crystals create a mysterious pool of light. There is a flight of steps leading up to private seating areas where sheer curtains form tents through which silhouettes of the guests inside can be seen like puppets of a shadow theatre.

A slim and striking young woman in a black lace jumpsuit is waiting for us at the bottom of the staircase. She bows as we approach.

"Hello, my name is Jessica and I'm your host tonight. This isn't a mirage," she says cheerfully. "It's a modern oasis."

"It's paradise," Lucien and Quinn recite and she laughs.

Jessica guides us up the steps to the only unoccupied tent at a far end of the mezzanine floor. As we ascend, Lucien dips his hand into the koi ponds that flow on both sides of the stairs.

"Alright, make that five things," Donny murmurs to Quinn.

As we take our seats, Jessica tells us that Isaac will be joining us shortly. She signals a waitress in the shortest micro-mini skirt to take our drink orders. Donny asks for rum on the rocks. Quinn orders an Old Fashioned. I settle for a gin and tonic. Lucien's order is a glass of milk with a splash of vodka. The girl makes a deep bow, revealing her cleavage, and hurries off.

Jessica closes the curtains around us, then pulls out a gem-encrusted cigarette lighter from her pocket to light the candle on the table. "Let's proceed to the main event," she says. "We offer two options. You can tell me your personal preferences and I'll curate a selection of girls for you, or I can just send in the entire line-up of available girls right now."

I cannot believe that I'm in a place like this.

"I cannot believe that I'm in a place like this," Quinn beams. She has been gleeful since Donny told her where we were going tonight. "How many girls do you have?"

"We have 50 available tonight."

"That's a decent number," Donny says. He looks dead serious, taking mental notes of every detail of the space. "I'd like you to handpick a girl for me. Let's see how good you are."

"Yeah, me too," Quinn says.

"Certainly," Jessica says. "What would you like?"

"I like a girl with short hair," Donny says. "Preferably with a mole on the lower part of her face. Give me a Zhang Ziyi type. I want her to have a good command of English so we're able to banter. It'd be nice if she can play the piano or some sort of musical instrument, and is a fan of Wes Anderson and Park Chan-wook films so that we have something in common to talk about."

Jessica is nodding at each request, and just when she thinks Donny is done, he adds, "Oh, I also want her to be a single child, just a little competitive with a tendency of not sharing but I don't want her to be spoilt."

Lucien and Quinn crack up but Jessica stays dead serious, repeating everything that Donny said back to him. He looks impressed. She then turns to Lucien. "What about you, sir?" she says.

"Do you have any Malay women here?" he says.

"Yes we do."

"Can I meet all of them?"

"Of course you may, sir."

Donny and Lucien catch each other's eye but neither of them says anything. When Jessica asks Quinn for her preferences, she replies, "I fancy you, actually."

A look of surprise flashes across Jessica's face but she hides it with a chuckle and a hand covering her mouth. "I'm flattered, but I'm sorry ma'am, I don't work here in that capacity."

"Well, I'll pay to have a drink with you," Quinn says. "Whatever happens after that is entirely up to the moment. Or are you afraid that you'll fall in love?"

Jessica bows apologetically. "I'm still on duty. I can't, unfortunately."

Quinn shrugs and leans back in her chair, inhaling from her vape. "Well, in that case, just bring me ten of your most popular girls. I've a feeling that you're one of them."

Jessic does not look at all displeased. Then she turns to me. "And what would you like, sir?"

"No one for me," I say, shaking my head. She looks surprised and asks me if I would like to take a look at the selection before making my decision but I refuse.

Donny waves it off and Jessica bows.

With perfect timing, the waitress parts the flap of our tent and enters with our drinks on a golden tray. Donny glances at his watch as the drinks are served. "Give us twenty-three minutes before sending in the girls," he instructs Jessica.

Jessica and the waitress bows again before leaving the tent. As soon as they are gone, Donny says with a frown, "This is prostitution."

"And with those words, the emperor proved that he was not hoodwinked by the trick of glamorous new clothes," Lucien says with a milk moustache.

When Jessica returns, she has an entourage of beautiful women dressed in cocktail dresses. They stand in a row, and at Jessica's command, they bow together and greet us. I have lost count of the number of times we have been bowed to since we arrived.

"Welcome to Paradise," they all say in perfect unison.

Donny checks the time. "Exactly twenty-three minutes," he says in approval before scanning the women in front of us. "So which one of them is mine?"

Jessica gestures to a slender young woman who steps forward and blows a kiss at him. "This is Alice from Vietnam. As requested, she is a single child with short hair, a mole on her left chin, pale-skinned with sharp cheekbones like Zhang Ziyi, has a degree in communication, used to play the guitar and loves *The Grand Budapest Hotel* and *Lady Vengeance*. Did I miss out anything?"

Donny's lips twitch. "No you did not, good job," he says.

Alice bites her lower lip, winks at Donny and bows before leaving the tent. Jessica claps once and three dark-skinned girls step forward. She informs Lucien that they are all of Malay descent and, without a moment's hesitation, he chooses the one in a bright-pink dress. She beams, blows a kiss and leaves the tent too.

"That was Sofia," Jessica tells Lucien.

"Sofia," he repeats after her.

"And then there were ten," Quinn says, reclining in her chair, hands behind her head. The ladies look demure as she takes her time, looking the women up and down. "Who wants to go to bed with me?" she finally asks.

The girls giggle as they all raise their hands up to the sky.

"That was a necessary clarification," Quinn says. "I'll take the second one to the left in red, and also the girl with the tied-up hair in green."

"Sky's from Thailand," Jessica introduces the girl in a red sequined shift, before pointing to the girl with a fashionable bun. "And Amy is from Singapore."

"Oh perfect, I was hoping to get someone local." Quinn is

genuinely happy.

The two girls blow kisses at Quinn before departing. The others bow and follow suit.

Jessica hands booklets to Donny, Lucien and Quinn. I assume that they are menus, and they are in a way. "So now is when we customise your experience even further," she explains. "Our outfit catalogue is for you to choose your girl's attire. As you can see, we have a wide selection aside from top-tier lingerie. We also have cocktail dresses, superhero costumes, kimonos and cheongsams, teacher and schoolgirl outfits and so much more. But aside from that, we also welcome you to select their personality type. They can be submissive, domineering, a girlfriend, an ex-girlfriend, a stranger's cheating wife, your boss, your principal, your stepsister or whoever you want. Half an hour from your order, I'll escort you to one of our opulent bedrooms upstairs where your girl or girls will be waiting for you. Of course, if you have any other special requests, please let me know."

"Special requests like...?" Donny asks.

Jessica smiles. "She's all yours for the night. You tell us what you want her to do and we will make that happen."

"I'd like something not in your catalogue," says Quinn.

Jessica replies without hesitation, "That can be arranged. What would you like Sky and Amy to be dressed as?"

"As you," Quinn answers.

Jessica is unfazed. "I will oblige."

Lucien timidly raises his hand. "Can you ask my girl to call me 'sayang'?"

"That will be no trouble at all. In fact, you can request for much more than that. Our girls are completely customisable to be exactly who you want them to be."

"Completely customisable," Lucien parrots, his brows knitting together as he absorbs the weight of her words.

"Precisely. For example, if you'd like the girlfriend experience, all you need to do is brief me on the history that you'd like you and Sofia to have. For example pet names and inside jokes, where you two went on your first date, how long you've been dating, who wears the pants in the relationship… you can choose the situation too. Is this your anniversary? Is she your best friend's girlfriend that you're secretly sleeping with? Perhaps you two just had an argument and are about to have make up sex? Whatever experience you want – we can provide to absolute perfection. Trust me, we can turn her into exactly what you'd want your girlfriend to be."

The more she talks, the further Lucien seems to retreat into himself. Then he stands up abruptly, as though suddenly waking up from a bad dream, startling everyone.

"Silly me, I forgot that I spilled something back home and I need to wipe it up before it leaves a stain," explains Lucien, excusing himself. He stands up to leave. "Please cancel my order – I mean that girl."

"Same here," says Donny.

"May I ask why?" Jessica asks in genuine surprise.

"I don't want to leave my friend here alone," he says, gesturing to me.

"Oh, don't worry. We will make sure that your friend is well taken care of while you are away. We can send down a masseur to him, or an iPad with Netflix TV shows, and some food and more drinks."

"I'm not in the mood," Donny interrupts. His lips are stretched thin.

At the look on Donny's face, Jessica realises that it would be best not to argue. She bows again before parting the curtain for Lucien.

"See you back at The Haven," he says, making his exit with Jessica following him.

Donny tosses the catalogue on the table, shaking in anger.

"This is revolting," he says.

"Yes, totally," Quinn grins, still flipping through the booklet in amusement. "Isaac has completely molested your soul."

"Is there a less disgusting way you could've phrased that?"

"Where's the fun in that?" Quinn says.

Jessica returns to escort Quinn to a bedroom. Quinn waves with both hands as she leaves. There is a forced smile on Donny's face.

Donny sits back, glaring straight at the now closed curtains. He is deep in thought. We remain silent. After a while, he leans forward and instantly snuffs the candle out with his thumb and finger.

"This is revolting," he says.

"You already said that."

"I'm shocked that Isaac thinks that the guests of The Haven would enjoy a place like this."

"I'm more shocked that you even agreed to come here."

Donny's outraged expression dissolves. "So you are disappointed in me."

"I'm just curious why you're doing this."

Donny sits back. "I think that I can help him," he says. "Not in the way that he wants, but in the way that he needs. And he will find it at The Haven. But he won't have agreed to come this weekend if I didn't show up here first. This was a necessity disguised as a courtesy."

"I see."

He looks at me appraisingly, slightly amused. "You seem unconvinced by my answer. Why do you think I did this?" he says.

Before I can respond, someone bursts through the curtains. I almost spill my drink. It is Isaac, dressed in a black suit and tie, wearing his smarmy look. "I'm so glad that you made it," he says to Donny, sitting down between us. "Too bad what's his name had to leave. But your other friend is upstairs with her girls, yes?"

"It would seem so," Donny says.

"Excellent," Isaac says, pulling the ashtray on the table closer. He opens his cigarette case and offers it to Donny and me. Donny takes a smoke. I refuse. "Oh, what a saint," he says absentmindedly before lighting up his cigarette and exhaling. "So you don't smoke and you don't like my girls. Why are you even here?"

Without waiting for a response, Isaac turns to Donny. "So! Mister hard-to-get, I heard that you picked a girl but changed your mind. Was she not up to standard?"

"No, she was very beautiful."

"Beautiful? Dude, she's hot as shit. She's on the house, go up and let her show you a good time. We can talk business after."

"No, we can talk business right now," Donny says, lighting up his cigarette and blowing out a steady stream of smoke. "I can go into details if you want me to, but for starters it is excessive how much your staff bow."

"What! Why?"

"I counted at least 20 times from the moment we arrived through the gate. The experience doesn't feel sincere."

Isaac laughs loudly. "Who cares about sincerity? I want my customers to feel like kings. The constant bowing tells my clients that they are powerful. And what do you think of Jessica? Isn't she the consummate hostess? She's great at customer relations."

Donny's lip curls. "Yes, she was superb. And you want me to take over her job?"

"Oh no, not at all. I'm perfectly satisfied with her," he says.

162

"If you think her customer service is good now, wait till she has her clothes off. I want you to be in charge of the entire front-end of The Paradise. I want you to teach my girls and staff how to seduce, charm and wrap my customers around their fingers. I can't think of anyone more suitable for this job than you."

I can see that Donny wants to tell Isaac off but he just stares at the cigarette in his hand as if it is the most toxic thing in the room. Isaac remains oblivious, the smug grin still on his face.

"So you don't need my contacts, then?"

"Oh, I definitely want that too," Isaac says. "Only a fool would say no to your network of rich and powerful people. But this is the priority. I need someone like you on my side."

Donny opens his mouth to speak, but remains silent. Even Isaac can now sense the hesitation. So, he places an arm around Donny like a long-lost brother. "I'd consider this a personal favour, my friend. You have no idea how much it'll mean to me if you say yes. I'm sure that you've already realised this, but The Paradise is almost entirely inspired by The Haven. All this wouldn't be here if it weren't for that amazing mind of yours. So I want you on board. Together we can create something brilliant."

The ash on the end of Donny's forgotten cigarette drops to the floor. Isaac keeps his eyes on the prize and to my shock, Donny smiles and shrugs. "I could consider it."

Isaac is ecstatic. He grips Donny by both shoulders and shakes him. "You beautiful bastard! You just made my entire year!"

"That's great."

Isaac snaps his fingers at me. "Oh yeah, you're a social media manager, right? What's your name again, Paul right?"

"His name's not Paul, Isaac – "

"You do up an Instagram page for The Paradise. I mean, something tasteful of course. Keep it subtle but alluring, so people are intrigued to find out more. Donny tells me that you're a wizard, so this should be a piece of cake for you."

"No thank you," I say.

Isaac takes a moment to comprehend my words. 'No' does not seem to be something that he is used to hearing.

"It'll be easy, dude," he insists. "Just pictures of our girls, some captions, hint to what we provide but don't disclose the location. How much do you usually get for your projects, I'm guessing $2K to $5K a month? I'll double it. No problem."

"No thank you," I say again.

"Why?"

"Because I don't want to."

He shrugs it off and rises to his feet. "You're right, it's probably better for The Paradise to remain inconspicuous. I've already banked $100k in the last three days anyway, no need to rock the boat. Let me get us a bottle of champagne to celebrate. I'll be right back, boys."

As Isaac leaves, Donny looks at me like I had just easily won the war that he has spent his entire life fighting.

"I don't think you're here because you want to help Isaac," I say. "I think it's because you feel like you need to. I have not met anyone more fascinated in people and wanting to unearth them than you. But some people aren't that complex. Isaac is just a narcissist. You don't have to help everyone, especially someone like him. You should keep your eyes on the people that you can lean on."

Donny keeps looking at me curiously before gingerly reaching over and cuffing me on the shoulder like he always does. He smiles, almost to himself, shaking his head. "Lucky you," he says.

When Quinn returns to the tent an hour later, Donny

hurries us out even though Isaac insists on popping open yet another bottle of champagne. At the entrance, Donny ignores the prattle of Isaac, snatches the keys from the valet's hands and speeds out of The Paradise. He is not in the least interested in Quinn's debrief on the girls and their customer service.

I am looking out the window at the passing buildings and nightlights. I hear Quinn ask, "Are we planning anything for Isaac this weekend? I'm assuming he's the VIP of the party."

I turn as Donny laughs, and he glances over at me. "No," he says. "I don't think he's worth it."

I can see Quinn's look of surprise from the rear-view mirror. "Well, something clearly happened while I was away," she says. "Care to share?"

"Where's the fun in that?" I say and Donny bursts out laughing.

"Quick. Let's act like nothing happened and everything is status quo. Sound good?"

The weekend comes and Zephyr and Donny meet for the first time at the entrance of The Haven. I told Donny that I was inviting someone, and he was not disappointed that it wasn't Caroline. Instead he looked elated, insisting on personally welcoming my guest to the party.

Zephyr arrives. I am in my bedroom, staring at myself in disbelief in the mirror. I had planned to wear a black T-shirt and sweatpants, but Donny somehow convinced me that it is imperative that I dress in what he has chosen for me. Much to my dismay, he dresses me up in a Lion King T-shirt and polka-dotted pyjamas pants.

When I finally come to terms with the get-up, I make my way downstairs, trying to ignore Lucien choking on his bowl of cereal at the sight of me. "Comic sans!" he yells. "Seriously?"

I hear Zephyr's laughter from the entrance. When I reach the ground floor, I see why.

Donny looks like a human rainbow. Nestled in his hair is a pair of bright orange sunglasses, mismatched with a lime green shirt, bright silver sweatpants and a pair of LED-light-up shoes.

"I want to applaud you for your effort, but I'm afraid that I'll miss my hands," Zephyr says and Donny lets out a

166

booming laugh. She is dressed in a Pikachu onesie, a lollipop in her mouth. "I'm too distracted by the traffic light that is your shirt."

The two of them see me approach and the lollipop falls out of Zephyr's gaping mouth.

"Oh my god, what on earth convinced you that this was a good look?" she says.

"That would be me," Donny grins. He reaches out his hand for a handshake and she takes it. "I'm Donny. It's a pleasure to have you here. Our mutual friend has told me absolutely nothing about you."

"I'm Zephyr, and I've heard plenty about you."

"Good things, I presume?"

"William isn't known for elaborating. But I'd say that you live up to what I thought you'd be."

"And what's that?"

"Someone who stands out like foie gras in a food court. But also someone who writes fan fiction about himself in his spare time."

Donny makes a happy face at me. "Oh, I like her," he says.

*

The Haven is buzzing. At the entrance, two voluptuous women dressed in lacy nighties welcome guests. In the lobby is a bed fitted with a colourful sheet and filled with psychedelic pillows. A flock of sheep made of neon cotton gambol overhead. Attractive guests in all manner of nightgowns and pyjamas take turns lying down to pose for Quinn and her camera.

Donny takes Zephyr by the hand. She is beaming from ear to ear as he guides her through the venue. The place looks like a wonderland to her as she soaks in the details. She notices that the ceiling lights have been strategically enveloped with cotton wool to look like dark clouds on the cusp of raining. She points out the servers offering champagne in baby bottles and animal-cracker shaped canapés. They are in pink shirts, white socks and tight briefs.

"Is that a throwback to Tom Cruise in *Risky Business?*" she asks Donny.

"Indeed!" he says, giving two thumbs up. "Madam Mischief will be overjoyed."

Zephyr looks across the room and sees a wall made of every conceivable type of cereal box. Lucien is standing in front of it, looking completely at home.

"That's such a nice touch," Zephyr says, impressed.

"No gold Honey Star for correctly guessing whose idea it was," says Donny. "Lucien just had to take this opportunity to show off his collection."

"What's the wifi password of this place?" I hear someone inquire from a server next to me.

"Have a conversation instead."

"Wow. Alright then."

"No, *haveaconversationinstead* is the wifi password."

"Oh, I see."

I spot Isaac standing between the candy floss and popcorn stands. He is dressed in a grey sharkskin suit. His arm is around the waist of the candy floss girl, whispering into her ear. He smirks as red surfaces on her face.

"Isaac's here," Donny says. "Excellent."

I'm still wondering why he was so adamant about inviting Isaac to tonight's party.

"Is he a friend of yours?" Zephyr asks. "Shouldn't someone tell him that he's not dressed in theme?"

"Maybe later when he has an audience," Donny says.

Wherever I look, something interesting is happening. In

one corner of the living room, hammocks hang from the ceiling in front of a wall display of sleeping hats. In another corner, people nestled in beanbags watch Christopher Nolan's *Inception* beamed from a projector on a wall. In the main area, people gather around two graffiti artists who are working their creativity on the DJ console that is shaped like a giant pillow. I notice that a lot of the guests have headphones on, each set lit up in apple green, tangerine or grape.

I can see Zephyr mentally taking down notes about every feature and how they all fit into theme, from the sets, to the costumes of the waiters, to the food served and the names of the cocktails. She is clearly impressed. She is pointing to everything, explaining to me how they all come into play with each other. Her enthusiasm is infectious, and my eyes stay on her.

"Which events company did this?" Zephyr inquires.

"None," I tell her. "Donny dreams it up and Quinn makes calls and it just happens."

"Oh wow!"

Donny grins at Zephyr. "I've a couple of guests later that I'd like to introduce you to. They're great potential clients for your events outfit. I hope you brought name cards."

Zephyr turns to me, surprised. I shake my head. "I didn't tell him what you do," I say.

She turns back to Donny who spreads his arms, palms up. "Yes, I'm awesome. All you need to know is that this place is a –"

He stops. Something has caught his attention. Not just him, others in the room have turned in the same direction. I look to see what the gazes are transfixed on and I should have guessed, it is not what but who – Caroline has arrived. She looks stunning wrapped in a silk midnight blue nightgown which ripples with her every step. She is carrying the waves of the dark ocean with her.

Isaac is watching her too. He looks ready to attack.

"The shark smells blood in the water," Donny says, noticing Isaac's hungry leer. Zephyr laughs at this reference to Isaac's suit. Donny cocks his head at Zephyr and me. "Let's give him his moment and see what he does with it," he says.

We approach Caroline. She smiles when she sees us.

"Hey, Melbourne boy," she says. "How's things?"

It is as though our date never happened and all that was shared were never said.

"Okay, and you?"

"On top of the world," she says, turning to Donny and Zephyr. "Very nice seeing you again, Zephyr. You are totally rocking that onesie! And Donny – amazing party, as always."

"And the sky is blue and the ocean is deep," he says and she laughs, clapping her hands together. "Let's make the night better with some tipples."

As we proceed to the kitchen, I see Isaac move as well. He follows us from across the room, leaving the disappointed-looking candy floss girl in his wake. He saunters through the crowd, coolly undoing the top few buttons of his collared shirt to reveal his well-sculpted chest. We reach the kitchen island, where others have gathered to watch the bartender flipping bottles and mixing cocktails, at the same time. It is here, at the makeshift bar, that Caroline and Isaac have their first conversation.

"I'm Isaac. Isaac Yong."

"Oh, I know who you are," Caroline says mischievously. "A couple of my girlfriends are in love with you."

"Are you not part of the equation?"

"You'll never hear it from me. I hold my cards close to my breast. I see you're not dressed according to theme."

He smirks and runs his palm down his jacket, stopping just

beyond his belt. "I happen to sleep naked. This is my birthday suit."

Donny and Zephyr's eyes widen as Caroline lets out a shriek of laughter. "You are horrible. Why on earth would you go through all that effort just for a bad joke?"

Isaac looks straight at her. "I guess to make someone like you laugh."

Caroline cups her chin and puts a finger to her lips and asks coyly, "Just that?"

"Let's say I'm a matador with the smoothest moves."

"Are you implying that Caroline is a bull?" Zephyr blurts out and I snort into my drink. "You know that bulls aren't being charmed, but irritated by the matador's outfit and movements, right?"

I catch Caroline glance over at Zephyr and flash her a grin.

"Speaking of irritants," says Isaac, directing his words at Zephyr, "it's nice that no one's harassing me tonight. So far, anyway."

Caroline intentionally takes the bait. "Who harasses you, Isaac?"

"Frankly speaking, I'm still a little embarrassed. I shouldn't talk about it."

"But clearly you'd like to, so why don't you?" Zephyr says but Isaac ignores her. His eyes are on Caroline, who gives him the response that he was looking for. So he begins to loudly tell his tale about wealth and popularity at a club last night. A despiser of any braggart, Zephyr summons her willpower to not burst out laughing. But Isaac's charm works on ladies nearby who turn in from their own conversations to eavesdrop and flutter eyelids. Isaac's gaze, however, remains fixed on Caroline. It is as though she is the only one in the room. Throughout the story she does not turn away, looking honestly captivated by his pigheadedness.

When he is done, Caroline gushes. "Well, aren't you something. Not many men can say that a woman crawled through a crowd on a nightclub dance floor just to pretend to bump into them."

"It was embarrassing, I tell you. I don't like attention. I'm sure that a ravishing woman like you experiences that on a daily basis."

"We're not talking about me, we're talking about you. What happened after she asked for your number? Did you give it to her?"

"I figured that she desperately wanted me to give it to her," Isaac says smugly and there is a ripple of laughter. "But then her friend did the most hilarious thing and –" Here Isaac pauses for effect. "I've said too much already."

"Oh no," Caroline says. "Finish your story! I want to hear it."

"Yes, do, please!" some woman says. Others nod hopefully.

Isaac scans his audience. "Well, if everyone's interested..."

"I'm interested," Caroline says, reeling him in. "Isn't that what matters?"

So Isaac continues. Caroline looks riveted by him, doe-eyed and fascinated; giving him all the reactions that one recounting such a story wants. Then unexpectedly, she reaches out causally and takes the drink from his hand, takes a sip and gives it back to him. It is a simple act but Isaac loses his train of thought mid-sentence and finds himself staring down at the lipstick mark on his whiskey glass, transfixed. Caroline pulls him back to earth by calling his name with a playful inflection, in a way he has never heard before. Then she smiles like she belongs to him and Isaac instantly loses all the words in his arsenal.

"Damn, she's good," Zephyr whispers to me.

Caroline follows up Isaac's story with one of her own, and now it is his turn to lean in, ask for details, intrigued and disarmed. And when she is done, he guffaws, laughing louder than the rest of us combined.

"You listen to Arctic Monkeys and The Black Keys!" Isaac says. He sounds astonished. "I'd never have imagined a girl like you would enjoy the same kind of music that I do. You're alright."

Caroline pretends to be scandalised. "Alright?" she says. "Out of all the words to describe myself, 'alright' would be the last one I'd use."

"I beg your pardon," Isaac genuinely apologises. "How would you describe yourself?"

Caroline tilts her glass towards him and Isaac instinctively reaches forward to touch her glass with his. Studying him sweetly, she coos, "I'm an orca."

Zephyr leans over and asks. "What did she mean by that?"

I cannot help but smile. "She's going to drown the shark," I say.

*

Caroline joins a few of her friends who have just arrived, with Isaac tailing in her wake. Donny leaves the two of us alone to welcome more of his guests to The Haven.

Zephyr and I wander over to the food wagons serving soft serve ice cream on doughnuts, sashimi sliced on the spot and pasta with mentaiko sauce. There are chairs shaped like Milo and Horlicks tins that people sit on and pose for photos together.

Zephyr goes to the bar and comes back sipping on her choice of pale ale. I surprise her by taking the bottle out of her hand and helping myself to a healthy swig. Her look of shock is so adorable that I take a couple more sips.

"That's drink number four, kehehe," she says. "Careful now."

"Nope. You've lost count, drunkie. This is but my drink number two."

It hits me in full velocity how much I missed her. It feels almost tangible, like a wallop. Zephyr with her strange laugh and passionfruit perfume – she is an antidote to chaos and all things foreign. If not for her, I would probably have wandered around for ten minutes, helped myself to the food before returning to my room. There is so much about Zephyr that is superlative, that the delayed reaction to her return in my life finally runs through me like a current of electricity.

People like Caroline and Donny, and yes, Isaac too, are entertainers. They gravitate to the limelight that put themselves in the heart of a crowd for as long as possible. Zephyr is more easily contented. She keeps her eyes on me. I do not deserve it in the slightest but here I am, in the middle of all that she sees. She does not need the crowd. I do not need it either. I have lived my whole life without being part of one. If the party ended at this moment, the music brought to a halt, the guests left to seek their next source of entertainment, I would be content with no one and nothing but Zephyr next to me.

As if my secret desires were audible, the crowd begins to disperse from around us. They go to the heart of the party where the band has begun to play. Neither Zephyr nor I are interested enough to get up, so we sit together under the fairy lights, listening to the music from a distance.

"Did Melbourne feel like this?"

"It wasn't this enjoyable."

"That's because I wasn't there," she nudges me playfully.

"I can't argue with that. It would be like trying to refute the law of gravity."

Zephyr purses her lips, as she so often does when trying to bite her tongue. I know what is held in reserve, and am grateful when she refrains from bringing it up. She takes a swig of the beer and gestures at me to finish it. I do as instructed.

"If you had to choose between Melbourne or here, where would you live?" she says.

"I'm fine with either."

"You have no preference?"

"It's like asking an alien if he feels more comfortable on a mountain or by the sea. Both are out of his comfort zone."

My best friend rolls her eyes at me. "You're not an alien, William."

"I know."

In the distance, the band finishes their set to the wild hoots and hollers of the crowd.

"Actually, Zephyr, I think I am."

The world's most colourful soul turns to me curiously.

"I've always been one. I washed up on shore and haven't found my footing since. I don't have a favourite dish. I don't like movies. I want to be alone but I'm lonely and tired. I'm sick of where I am but I don't want to leave. I feel misplaced and it sucks. I hate it. I feel shipwrecked."

"This is the alcohol talking, electric eel."

"No, it is not."

Zephyr places her hand over mine. I turn it over and she entwines our fingers and smiles brightly, brighter than anything in the world.

"People get lonely. But they're never alone. And as long as I'm here, you're going to be neither."

I want to kiss her. It is a curious sensation, what I am going through. I want to pull her close and kiss her and never let go, but with almost as much yearning, I want to tell her how much I missed having her by my side. Before I have a chance to make my choice, Donny lopes towards us, one arm swinging, the other clutching a bottle of champagne. He has headphones hung around his neck.

"Look at the two of you, out here by your lonesome. Just about as innocent as a married man's Tinder profile," he hollers.

"You look like the last person I want to see in the bouncy castle of a kid's birthday party. Are you here simply to ruin our moment?" Zephyr retorts and Donny pulls a cheeky face.

Donny reaches us and holds out the champagne. I clink it with the beer bottle. "Come and dance. The silent disco is up next."

It is an intriguing concept. Three DJs control the music from their individual consoles, and listeners are invited to switch among the three channels throughout the night from their headphones. The DJ who receives the loudest cheers is determined the winner. The green headphones play old-school classics. The orange ones play EDM and mainstream music, which seems to please the crowd the most. Donny is grooving vigorously to it. As for the purple headphones, the music is erratic. One moment it plays Top 40 hits, transitions into Disney tunes and suddenly jumps to K-Pop.

Zephyr and I follow Donny to the dance floor but stop short of joining him in the centre. Instead, we linger together, amusing ourselves by watching the crowd belt out different songs and cheer at different moments. A server comes over and offer us headphones. I decline, but Zephyr gives me a look and takes two pairs for us.

Like Donny, most of the crowd is tuned to the orange DJ. At the chorus, everyone lets out a whooping cheer and sings along, spreading arms upward and outward, curling towards each other, in an arc to the side and making an apex. I stick with the green, which is now playing "Superstition" by Stevie Wonder. Zephyr goes with the purple, which almost nobody is listening to. The DJ spots her and gives her a thumbs up.

"That's awkward, I was about to change to a different DJ," she murmurs and I laugh.

At the other end of the room, Isaac is whispering feverishly into Caroline's ear. She shakes her head and says something to him. Whatever it was, it has resounding impact. He pulls her by the arm. She looks surprised, then cups his cheek in her hand and makes her way to the dance floor where a circle immediately forms around her. Isaac remains in a corner watching Caroline, a mixed look of resentment and fascination on his face. She has him spellbound and he hates himself for it. I wonder what she said to him.

Zephyr and I find ourselves in a corner of the dance floor at the edge of the large circle of revellers in which Donny and Caroline are dancing. We are still listening to different music but dance to the same rhythm, her hips rocking against mine.

Caroline has started a bunny hop across the dance floor as Donny gyrates furiously. Zephyr is saying something to me. I cannot quite hear her but from reading her lips, she is telling me that she missed me. So, I say aloud: "I missed you too."

She smiles at me like I am the only one in the world who matters. It is a smile that makes my heart ache and makes me want to give in to the evening's atmosphere. Zephyr shuts her eyes and grooves to the music, swaying her body. Before I realise what I am doing, I lean in and kiss her.

Nothing ever works out the way it does in movies – I can feel her freeze up against me. As I pull away, I see that she is looking at me strangely. She pulls off the headphones. I follow suit.

"Why did you do that?" she says, in a voice not quite like her own.

In a past, I would have claimed temporary insanity due to inebriation or stood in front of her mutely.

"I'm sorry, I won't do it again."

"Don't be sorry. I just need to know why you did it."

"Because I wanted to."

"Because you... wanted... to."

There is bitterness in the way she says that, and I feel that I have ruined something sacred. I am looking everywhere from the bead of sweat on her forehead to the glowing headphones on her shoulders to the bumping crowd behind her. I am looking at anything, anywhere, but there is no escape. Finally I meet her eyes, and find myself transported.

I am back on the plane. There I am, ready to land in Singapore after a long hiatus. I am the only passenger awake on the entire aircraft. The flight attendant leans over across the sleeping passenger next to me, rests her hand on my shoulder and tells me to put my safety belt on and prepare for landing. There is that familiar jittery feeling, the sensation of butterflies in my stomach, as I peer out the window to look at the cityscape from the wingtip. The plane tilts downward, banking, ready to land.

The glowing city below looks like a birthday cake ready to be blown out. It looks more alive than I have ever seen it. There I hover above, in an awkward metallic creature descending from the clouds.

"Ladies and gentlemen, we have the most important announcement in the world," the captain's booming voice blares over the speaker to the sleeping passengers. "The electric eel is coming home."

Zephyr's next words bring me back to the blistering ulcer that is my reality. "I'm engaged, Will."

Behind us, the people on the dance floor lets out a loud cheer to the music.

It feels like a sledgehammer has hit me. What follows immediately after is incredible numbness. When I kissed my best friend, I was in the heat of the moment, but now it feels like I did the world's most heinous thing.

My throat has run dry and my voice comes out in a hoarse croak. "How long ago was this?"

Zephyr looks visibly upset. No more forced laughter. My kiss has done her a great disservice. She looks like she is about to cry. "About six months ago," she says.

"AND I SAID MAYBEEEEEEE..." Donny bellows, cutting in with an impressive level of musical insensitivity. "YOU'RE GONNA BE THE ONE THAT SAVES ME!"

"And after all..." The crowd joins in, swaying to the music. Some of them switch on their phone flashlights and lift them up high. The other two DJs turn to each other and shrug sheepishly. Everyone on the dance floor has tuned in to the music from one console, their headphones all flashing a brilliant green.

"YOU'RE MY WONDERWALL!"

Zephyr pulls away from me. "I'm sorry, Will. I've wanted to tell you for the longest time, but I could never find the right moment to do it. Please don't hate me. You're my best friend in the entire world."

There it is. Zephyr's forced smile. It tears my heart to shreds.

I see her slowly drift out of reach even though she has not stepped an inch away from me. Watch me ruin everything; watch me make the good things in my life disappear whenever I open my mouth. I don't like this. It feels too familiar. It feels like goodbye.

"Rewinding cassette tapes always leave marks. I think that there's symbolism there somehow."

"You're going back to Melbourne?"

Last night's party had heightened Lucien's craving for breakfast food. Cradled in his hands is a cereal bowl so big that I could fit my face in it. It is exploding with colours of Honey Stars, Coco Crunch, Lucky Charms and Blueberry Morning swirling in chocolate milk.

"But you just got here!" he says, as Quinn ends her phone call. "Why do you have to leave?"

"I've overstayed my welcome. It's time that I returned to reality."

"What does that even mean?" Lucien scratches his head. "The escape of reality is what makes living so interesting. So, if meaning is what you're searching for, I can promise you that –"

"Did something happen during last night's party?" Quinn interrupts. "Please tell us if someone did something to you. We'll make sure he or she never steps foot in here again."

"No one did anything," I say. "I just need to go."

Donny does not seem to share Quinn and Lucien's surprise. He is finishing the apple in his hand, calmly scrolling through his iPad. "Did you not enjoy yourself last night?" he says, not looking up from the screen.

I had the time of my life, Donny. But true to form, I blew it.

"It was great as always. Anyway, I'm sorry about the business connections that you've sent my way. I promise to continue handling their social media channels from Melbourne."

"That is the last thing on my mind right now and you know it," Donny says firmly. He takes one last bite of his apple before tossing the core into a bin. "Is there anything you'd like to tell us?"

No, Donny. Of course there isn't.

My silence invites Quinn and Lucien to guess the reason for my departure. They each have theories that grow increasingly wild as they speculate.

"Something must have triggered this," Quinn says, looking around the room as though trying to recall who was where last night. "Was there someone with an Aussie accent around? Or did one of the movies screened last night have Hugh Jackman or Nicole Kidman in it? Or was it those chairs shaped like Milo tins? Milo was created in Australia – my mother told me that. Wait! Is it your mother? Is she sick? Do you need to go home and take care of her? No that can't be right – if that were the case, Donny would've interrupted by now."

Donny keeps his eyes on me but says nothing. I have a feeling that he already knows the truth, or is at least dangerously close to it. I feel a rush of gratitude for his silence.

"Is it because you still feel foreign to the colours and vibrations of this space?" Lucien says. "Because the soul is a funny thing. It calibrates at its own pace. Just because you feel like you don't belong somewhere doesn't mean you have to leave it. Am I right? Is that what's troubling you?"

Quinn pounds the table with a closed fist, startling both Lucien and me. "I got it. It was Isaac, wasn't it? He was acting like a complete lovesick puppy last night. Did he intimidate you because he realised how much Caroline likes you? I'm guessing he cornered you and threatened you with – "

"No, he was never alone last night," Lucien says before his voice falters. "Whenever I looked over, I saw – "

"That's enough, guys," Donny says quietly. The two of them turn to him curiously as he finally looks up from his iPad. "If he doesn't want to tell us why he's leaving, we shouldn't force him to."

Lucien looks at Donny in amazement before hanging his head.

"I cannot believe you just said that," Quinn says. "Why aren't you upset by this?"

"I am upset," Donny says, turning to me, his voice emanating warmth. "You're not being held hostage here. Leave as and when you want. But we're here if you need someone to lean on."

I nod my head numbly. "Thank you, Donny."

Lucien looks like he's on the edge of saying something else to persuade me to stay but holds back. Instead, he offers his box of cereal. "Do you want some breakfast?" he asks.

"Thanks, Lucien," I say.

"I'll get the milk," Quinn adds with a sigh, her hands in the pockets of her modern kimono.

"Thanks, Quinn."

*

Back when I was in Melbourne, I frequently ate cereal before bed. I never had it for breakfast, strangely enough. I only enjoyed eating cereal at night. One evening, I opened the fridge to find that I had run out of milk. So I went to the convenience store to buy a carton. At the checkout counter, there was a middle-aged gentleman paying for cigarettes, and a young man in a suit behind him holding a bouquet of flowers.

When it came to the young man's turn, he shambled groggily forward. The cashier said, "Hey mate, how's it goin'?" obviously expecting the reflexive response of, "not too bad, yourself?"

"HORRIBLE. MY HEART IS IN DECAY, LACHLAN," the young man bellowed, reading off the cashier's nametag. He then began expressing his sadness with grand gestures, waving the bouquet of flowers about.

He was on internship in Sydney and was back for the weekend to surprise his girlfriend. It was their three-year anniversary. When he returned to their apartment, he found her in bed with his ex-footy teammate. Lachlan froze as the young gentleman began slapping the bouquet on the counter in percussive rhythm.

I knew why Lachlan was at a loss. He had not expected such honesty. The social contract stipulates that concern is not required between strangers. Maintain the obligatory façade of friendliness, and you will not be met with resistance. Yet, here was this young man, baring his soul, so he did not know how to react.

Fortunately for Lachlan, he did not have to suffer long. The young man's soliloquy had come to an end. Winded and in tears, he stumbled out of the store, stomping carelessly on the petals that now littered the floor.

I stepped up to the counter with my carton of milk. Lachlan looked hesitant, afraid to ask how my day was. "Just the milk, then?"

"I'm eating cereal," I responded, somewhat lamely.

He looked relieved by the monotony of my answer.

"That wasn't foolish, what that guy did," I said to him. "I thought that he was brave."

*

I call my mother that evening. Her live-in boyfriend Gary picks up the phone. He tells me that she is in the shower.

"It's alright then. Never mind about it."

"Hold on, I'll tell her."

"Wait, that's not necessary – "

"Hey honey, it's your son on the line. I'll tell him to call you back later, alright?"

"NO YOU SHALL NOT!"

There is a burst of sound and not before long Gary's calm voice is replaced by my mother's anxious tone.

"Hey! It's Mom here. You never call me. This is either horrible news or amazing news. What happened? Are you alright? Is everything okay? Are you hurt? Are you sad? Are you happy? Talk, son."

"For God's sakes, let me get you a towel," says Gary from behind her.

"I'm fine, mom. I just wanted to hear your voice."

"No one wants to hear my voice. Not even Gary wants to hear my voice. Isn't that right, Gary?"

"I – "

"What happened? Tell me why you're calling or else I'm booking a flight to Singapore right now."

"That would be counterproductive," I say. I suddenly wish that I were on an old telephone receiver so that I could curl the phone line in my finger. I fidget with the table instead. "I'm going back to Melbourne."

My statement is met with silence, and I can almost hear the wheels in my mother's head turning. Then her shrill voice lowers to something wonderful and almost maternal.

"Did something happen, baby?"

"Nothing happened. I just want to go back."

"It can't be Zephyr. Her posts on Facebook are normal but some guy named Ashely keeps commenting and commenting but that's hardly –"

"Mom, please drop it. Can I stay with you and Gary when I'm back? I promise to move out once I find work."

"Of course you can," Gary says.

"Don't invite my son to your house without my say, Gary!" she snaps at him.

"Can you please put this towel on?"

"I've no time for towels, Gary. My son, my child, my egg, is heartbroken right now."

"I'm not heartbroken, Mom. I just want to go home."

There is a pregnant pause, then I hear my mother's deep sigh. "I think you're already home, son," she says. "I don't know what happened but this sounds like a reaction, not a decision. I am your mother. I know such things. In all honestly, I expected you to eventually tell me that you found a job there and decided to move back into our old flat."

"Everything I have is back in Melbourne, Mom."

"Are you sure about that?"

When I say nothing, my mother laughs. "When you followed me to Australia all those years ago, I asked if there was anything you were leaving behind. You said 'no' right away. I knew you were lying to me then, and I know you're lying to me now. Aren't you tired of running away? Kind of like when you were a kid, always looking for an escape – hey do you remember that playground I used to always bring you to? It was just behind the Chinese tuition centre you used to go to every Wednesday after school. There was this giant Angsana tree that you always tried to climb up even though you'd always get bitten by –"

"It didn't bloom, Mom," I tell her and she instantly falls

silent. She knows exactly what I am trying to say. The words come out of my mouth before I can catch them in the back of my throat. They hang in the air uselessly. I feel my cellphone shake in the palm of my hand. "I promise I actually tried but it didn't."

I hear her sigh again but I know that she is smiling. "If you want to come back, of course you'll be welcomed with open arms. My son can stay with us, can't he, Gary?"

"Yes, of course he can."

I can feel her tenderness through the receiver. "Are you still there?" she says.

"Yes I am, Mom."

"Good boy. My son's a majestic, eclectic warrior jellyfish that is circling the depths of the proverbial ocean that is boring society."

"What?" I say.

"What?" echoes Gary.

"And he deserves the world too. You deserve the world and the moon. Are you eating well?"

"Yes."

"Are you changing your underwear and socks every day?"

"Yes."

"Are you sleeping well? Have you been making a lot of nice friends?"

"Yes."

"Good. I want you to rest well tonight. Take a shower, say a nice prayer and go to sleep. Who knows what will happen when you wake up. Maybe you'll realise you changed your mind. Maybe you'll know for sure that you don't belong. Come back only if you've no reason to stay. Do that for me?"

"Sure, Mom."

"Good boy. Best boy. I can't wait till my son realises that he's so much more than just a pretty face."

"Sorry."

I do not sleep a wink that night. I toss and turn, my pillow feeling like a brick under my head. 12 am becomes 3 am. 3 am becomes 6 am. Soon light streams in from the windows and the streets below buzz with action but I stay rooted under the covers. I feel at odds with the world. It is not the first time that I have felt this way, but on this particular morning the mood is so strong that I feel that wakefulness is forcing me to stay restless in bed. You can't escape the fight today, I hear a voice repeatedly say to me. You can't escape the fight.

I wipe the sweat off my brow and shut my eyes for a moment to nurse my splitting headache. When I open them again something has changed. I am no longer in my bedroom. I'm in a classroom, but not just any classroom. Judging by the way the desks are placed, the colour of the whiteboard and the scenery outside the window, I can tell that this is where I used to go to in secondary school.

There is no one in the classroom but me. The lights are switched off, and everything is completely still except for the whirring of fan blades above. Then suddenly the lights flicker on, and the rest of the ceiling fans switch on. I hear a sudden sound of someone shifting in his chair next to me and I turn my head. Donny is grinning at me.

He is dressed in our old school uniform. He's not stocky anymore but pencil-thin, his hair spiked up excessively like a cockatoo. He looks exactly like how I remember him when we were kids.

Suddenly there is a loud ringing sound in the room. A phone has appeared out of nowhere in my open palm. I glance down at it. It's Zephyr. Her name glows on my phone's screen in big block letters. I sit there waiting for the shrill noise to stop. The room eventually goes quiet but within seconds the phone starts ringing again. I hastily turn the phone to silent and stuff it into my pocket. Donny shakes his head at me.

"You're not going to talk to her?" he says.

I don't know what to say to her.

"This is your subconscious, you know that means I can hear your thoughts, right?" Donny says. He looks around the classroom. "Perhaps you need a couple more friendly faces to weigh in."

At his words, Quinn, Lucien and Caroline appear at the desks around us. Caroline gives a whistle as she surveys the space.

"Is this is where you used to go to school?" she says. "The chairs are soooo short. I can't even dangle my feet."

This is so bizarre.

"Not as bizarre as you waiting years before kissing that girl again," Quinn says. "She's got dreamboat eyes and the perfect jawline. Ask her if she'd like to model for me. You know what, maybe I'll ask her myself. How about you hand over that phone to me real quick?"

Caroline touches me on the shoulder comfortingly and I do not move away. "How are you holding up?" she says.

"'How are you being weighed down?' is a more apt question," Lucien says. He is rocking back and forth in his chair, hands under his thighs.

188

I notice my schoolbag on the floor next to me. It is huge in comparison to the others'. Donny's is floral with a mirror on the front. Caroline's is a clutch handbag. Lucien's is a plastic bag and Quinn's is a camera sling bag. Mine almost looks like luggage. Looking closer, it actually is.

"So why have we been summoned here?" Quinn says. She is twirling a tube of lipstick between her fingers. "I assume that it is important."

"Yes it is. We are here to brainstorm for our conversationally challenged protagonist," Donny says, a whiteboard marker appearing in his hand as he approaches the front of the classroom. "Class is in session. Let's say that he manages to gather up the courage to pick up the phone. What should he say to her? There are no wrong answers."

"Whatever you're wearing right now would look better on my bedroom floor," Quinn says.

"Except for that," Donny says witheringly. But he proceeds to write it down on the whiteboard.

"Whatever you say, I don't think that you should apologise for kissing her," Caroline says, rubbing her chin thoughtfully.

Lucien turns to her. "That's colourful insight from the most beautiful woman in Singapore. May I ask why?"

"Because it's what you wanted. It's what she wanted too. She looked like she wanted to kiss you back."

How did you even know? You weren't there.

"I'm in your head, remember?" she says. "I don't blame her in the slightest, you look like you've got the softest lips."

"So you two actually didn't kiss?" Donny says, gesturing to Caroline and me.

"Not for lack of trying," Caroline says. She pulls a cigarette out of thin air. "Can I smoke in here?"

"Best not to," Lucien advises. "It's foggy enough as it is."

It appears that I was mistaken. What I thought was a tube

of lipstick in Quinn's hand is actually her vape. She draws it close to her mouth but rather than sucking on it, she uses it as though it is a dictation device.

"I want you to leave him for me," she says. "We're perfect for each other."

"Are you talking as our protagonist or as Madam Mischief?" Donny asks as he writes it down.

The whiteboard is filled up with words from the pleading to the desperate to the frustrated to the maddeningly sincere. But none of them seems to fit. Silent in my seat the entire time, I rise to my feet and walk to the whiteboard. Donny passes the marker to me and returns to his seat. My fingers touch the words and move in a downward motion. The words will not come off but my fingers are stained red.

"What matters is that you let her know how much you appreciate her," a voice says behind me. I turn. My mother has taken over my seat. She cocks her head at me. "She's dismayed. She thinks that she has lost you forever. She's fighting to keep you in her life."

"Is this your mom?" Quinn says, pointing. "She's hot."

"That is wildly inappropriate," Lucien says.

"Not in the slightest," my mother beams.

I don't deserve Zephyr fighting for me. Don't any of you understand? I've been nothing but a burden to her. She deserves better.

"We can hear you, my friend," Quinn intones, inhaling her vape and exhaling a long stream of smoke. The scent of passionfruit makes me numb.

"And I think that's up to her to decide," my mother says, as the others bob their heads in agreement. "It's arrogant of you to think otherwise."

I look down at my feet, scratching my head in frustration and when I look back up, the whiteboard has been wiped clean and all that remains is the beautiful name of my best friend in that brilliant scrawl that is her handwriting. I turn around and all my companions are gone. Zephyr is sitting three chairs away from me, a tired expression on her face. She's not on a classroom chair like the others were. She sits on a park bench in the middle of the classroom, dressed in a beautiful cheongsam like the first day we met.

"This is very dramatic of you," she says.

"I have a very theatrical imagination."

"I know that. Are we going to stay here long?"

"As long as you like to."

"Well, at least you're giving me a choice for once in this funny relationship of ours," she says, meeting my eye from across the room. "Are you really going to let me leave?"

"I have to."

She forces her trademark smile. It makes me want to burst out crying. "You just swallowed, William," she says.

When I open my eyes, I'm out of the classroom and back in my bedroom in The Haven, drenched in sweat and completely alone.

*

At 8:12 am there is a knock on my door. I try to ignore it, so the knocking persists. It begins to transition into a drumbeat. I recognise it as "Smooth Criminal" by Michael Jackson. I let it go on, and to my alarm the knocker begins to sing in a disturbing high-pitched voice like an insect's mating call. I groan, unable to ignore it any longer.

"Yes, what is it?" I say, doing a time check. It is 8:16.

"Oh, did I wake you?" It's Lucien's voice from the other side of the door. "There's someone here to see you. She's adamant not to leave."

191

I mentally calculate if there is the slightest possibility that my mother hopped on a plane and flew here to hug me.

"Is she old?" I say.

"Old enough to kick this door down," comes Zephyr's voice.

I make my way to the door and open it. Zephyr and Lucien are standing outside. Zephyr is wearing her work clothes – a white blouse with a Mandarin collar buttoned all the way up matched with black jeans. She is wearing glasses.

We head downstairs to the living room and the awkwardness is palpable. As the silence draws out, a giant grey animal with tusks and a trunk appears. It sits itself in the living room, taking up all the space as it flaps its floppy ears.

Lucien is chirpy. "Could I prepare something for the both of you? Coffee? Tea? Something with alcohol perhaps?"

I shake my head so he turns to Zephyr. "Would you like some tea?"

"No, I'm fine."

"Breakfast, perhaps? I'm an excellent cook."

"No thank you."

"Maybe something simple like *kaya* and butter on toast. Or how about half-boiled eggs with pepper and soy sauce?"

"No, really, we're fine."

He takes an ashtray and places it in front of Zephyr. "I saw you smoking a cigarette outside The Haven just now. Please feel free to light up."

"Thank you, that's very kind of you."

"I'll leave the two of you alone then," Lucien says, patting the creature on its broad rump.

"What an interesting, friendly guy. He was telling me just now about my air." Zephyr says after Lucien has retreated to his room and shut the door.

"Yeah he does that."

Zephyr attempts to feed the elephant some peanuts. "I've

left you over twenty missed calls. Were you planning to return at least one of them?" she demands.

I do not know what to say.

"So anyway, I have work in an hour but I said that I'd be late. Can we talk?"

"I have a lot of work to do."

"Is that so?"

"Yes."

"Let's make a list."

"What?"

"Let's list everything you have to do that is so urgent that it supersedes a conversation with your best friend who has travelled all the way here for you. Let's do it. I have paper and a pen."

She reaches into her sling bag but takes out cigarettes instead. When she places a stick between her lips and lights up, her hands are trembling.

She takes in a deep breath and says, "I'm sorry about that." Her words are shrouded in smoke.

No, you do not need to apologise at all. I'm the one who should be sorry. I'm so sorry.

"It's alright."

She flicks ash into the ashtray. "Can we talk about it?" she asks.

I am silent until she finishes her cigarette. She stubs the butt in the ashtray and sits upright.

"I know that you never liked the fact that I smoked. The way you'd scrunch up your nose when the fumes wafted in your direction, or the way you'd scratch your nose to hide your disdain whenever I lit up."

I hate the smell of cigarette smoke. I can't imagine a person on earth who enjoys it. But it smells like perfume coming from you.

Still, Zephyr lights up another cigarette. Her fingers twitch. I can tell that she wants me to open up, but how can I? I did and look what happened. It's the same old story. Nothing good ever comes of me sharing what's in my head.

I already know how this will end. There is no way we can banter our way out of this. She smokes her second cigarette in this silence as I stare down at our feet. I want to say something, anything, something brilliant, something comforting, anything at all, and I am racking my brain so hard that I can feel it ache. What comes out surprises me.

"Is it Ashley?"

"What?"

"Your fiancé. Is it Ashley?"

At first, Zephyr looks like she wants to burst out laughing. But then at the look on my face, her face falls. "Wow, you're actually serious. You think that I'd want to spend the rest of my life with someone like him? Do you even know me?"

"I was just asking. It's a simple question."

"It's a simple question and it has an obvious answer especially to someone who knows me like you do."

You're right. That was a stupid thing to ask.

I look back down at my feet.

"The answer is no, just to make it crystal clear."

You're right, Zephyr, I know there was no way you'd be with him. Why on earth did I even ask that? I messed up again. I don't even know why I said that. I should always keep my mouth zipped up.

"I need to go to work soon, Will," Zephyr says, glancing at her watch. She is trying to hide her impatience; I know she is. "You know I'd never force you to do anything, but can you please tell me how you feel?"

I'm back in the classroom again. I'm all alone. The place is in ruins, as though it was wrecked by a typhoon in my absence.

The ceiling has been blown clean off, debris is everywhere and everything from scattered chairs to torn up textbooks is caked with dust. In the centre of all the devastation sits the park bench, defiantly. I approach it, hesitating before the exhale as I reach forward to press my fingers on its cool steel.

"Will?" she says, with just the slightest hint of urgency. "Please say something before I go. Anything at all."

At this point there seems like nothing needs to be said but I say it anyway. I say the first thing that comes to my head and feel foolish as soon as it escapes my mouth.

"I wish I didn't leave you," I say.

Zephyr's eyes widen before she nods her head.

"I wish you stayed too," she says.

"This is the Frankenstein's monster of desserts."

Later that morning, Caroline shows up at The Haven. Donny, Lucien, Quinn and I are in the midst of having breakfast when she joins us at the kitchen island. She carries the aura of someone who has just won a war, glowing and triumphant. Lucien and her meet eyes for the first time ever. "I have a question to ask," she starts.

"Yes, you're the most beautiful human being I have ever seen," he says.

Caroline looks surprised, laughing as she draws a stray hair behind her ear. Donny greets her. "Good morning, love. Would you care for some *laksa*? Lucien has made plenty so grab yourself a bowl."

"I was wondering if we could discuss my favour from you."

Donny and Quinn do an elaborate handshake, one grin ending with the other. Donny says, "Madam Mischief and I have already started organising your event. When we're done with breakfast, I'll show you what we have in mind. We are aware of how much this means to you, so we planned it to the best of our capabilities – which I'm sure you already know, is extremely high."

Caroline laughs again. "Well, I'm very grateful. But I have something else that I'd like to ask of you."

"Another favour?" Donny says, pretending to look scandalised.

"Well, as I told you before, my event will centre around strangers getting on a stage to talk freely about things close to their hearts."

"And you're afraid that they'll be hesitant to get the ball rolling so you want me to be the first person to take the microphone," Donny says in a matter-of-fact way. "Of course I'll do it."

Caroline is delighted. "You're awesome!"

"Yes, I'm awesome. Would you like me to impress you again?"

"Go on then."

"You'd like your darling Melbourne boy to get on stage as well."

"Damn, you are so good," she says. They both turn to me expectantly.

I reject her request faster than it is socially acceptable. Caroline bites her bottom lip and asks me why I'm breaking her heart like this. I tell her that it is because I hate the limelight.

"What a terrible way to live," Donny says as I quickly return to my food to avoid succumbing to her gaze. "Caroline, you have my word. Not only will The Haven and my entire list of personal contacts be at your disposal, I shall be your first speaker."

"You're a darling. If you could somehow convince this boy here to join in the fun – "

"Done."

"Done?"

"It's already done."

"I'm delighted."

I look up from my *laksa*. "I'm sorry, what?" I say.

*

I eat *ice kachang* that afternoon. The auntie gets annoyed as I stand in front of her store deliberating about the fillings I want. The customer behind me is tapping his foot impatiently. I turn and ask him to recommend something, and he stares at me as if I am a leech reaching out to him.

So, I turn back to the *ice kachang* auntie and ask her to give me everything. She responds with an eloquent, "ha?"

I repeat myself. I want *ice kachang* with a bit of everything. I want the most comprehensive, strangest concoction that she has to offer. I am looking to devour the Frankenstein's monster of *ice kachang*.

With the same blank expression on her face, she repeats what I said. I nod. I want everything. The black grass jelly, the white sago balls, the red beans, the green flour worms, the yellow sweet corn, the pink agar-agar, the brown sea coconut, the translucent palm seeds, and whatever else that she has to offer. If she has leftover breadcrumbs or Milo powder, why not – heap it on as well.

The mini mountain she brings to me is an intimidating sight to behold. The auntie tells me that the *ice kachang* is enough for two to share. I ignore her and address it with great resolve.

I mine into the dessert from the top down. I chop into the ice shavings that have hardened into an icy coat. The first few spoonfuls are bland, the coating of milk and syrup having seeped well below the surface. I dig. I do not like the taste of the sea coconut and corn, but I persevere. I sample the black and green bits and cast them aside. I go deeper, encountering mouthfuls of colours and strange textures. There are all variants of cloying sweetness. I start feeling ill but driven by something I cannot quite describe remain determined to power through.

As the ice melts, a pool forms at the bottom of the bowl like sludge. Bits of the myriad ingredients float in it. With a deep breath, I lift the bowl up to my lips and glug it down.

When I set the bowl down, I see an intensely coloured slushy mound. It looks like it is glowing, almost shimmering, like treasure hiding under the seabed.

I pick up my spoon and scoop. The ice gives way effortlessly revealing the trove of red bean, *attap chee* and agar-agar hidden within. I eat. The flavours are rich and harmonious, the textures a wonder of contrasts. It is delicious in its simplicity. What comfort it is, this hidden treasure.

I finally see why Zephyr loves *ice kacang*.

"Until someone makes me realise otherwise, I'll forever assume I am not."

When night falls, Lucien and I head out for a drink. He picks a bar that is on the second floor of a warehouse in the middle of nowhere. Above its entrance is a Chinese signboard with the words "Uncle Tan's Kopitown" on it. It is dimly lit with buffed metal walls plastered with posters of Shanghainese glamour girls and decorated with shelves of vintage typewriters, lamps and telephones.

Lucien chooses a table underneath a row of 1960s mechanical toys. As we sit, a pretty bartender wearing a buttoned up shirt with embroidered peonies on the sleeves walks over and pats Lucien on the back jovially.

"Lucky Lu!" she says. "I haven't seen you for a while, what's been going on? What are you doing here? How've you been?"

"You have many questions, so I hope that this answer will be sufficient for all of them. I am sad tonight."

"I'll fix that," she says cordially. "Who's your handsome friend?"

"He's my soon to be ex-housemate," Lucien says solemnly before gesturing to her. "Meet the best bartender in town, Eden. Can you fix us up some cocktails?"

"I most certainly can, friend. What are you hankering for?"

I look around for a menu and she laughs.

"Everything here at Uncle Tan's Kopitown is bespoke. Just tell me what you feel like and I'll whip up something tasty."

"Give me something with sake in it," Lucien says. "But not too sweet, give me something bitter but pleasant. Add in some fruit."

Eden gives him a thumbs up, and turns to me. "What about you?"

"Umm... I don't know. How about you decide for me?"

"Oh no, that takes the fun out of mixology," she shakes her head at me before turning to Lucien. "Help me out here buddy. How would you describe your friend?"

Lucien thinks for a second. "He's a complex man with simple tastes," he says.

Eden grins and shoots finger guns at us. "I love that. Let's see what I can whip up for the both of you. Any snacks?"

"Yes. Give us some *har cheong* wings, your signature salted egg yolk popcorn and fried wantons."

"Gotcha. I'll be with you in a tick."

She leaves and Lucien sinks into the soft sofa, his eyes scanning the details of the room. "This is my favourite place in Singapore."

"Don't let Donny catch you saying that."

Lucien chuckles but says, "I'm very upset today."

"I'm sorry."

"Oh, you're only part of the reason. Honestly speaking, I kind of knew that someone with your personality wouldn't be at The Haven for long. Heck, I didn't think that I'd stay at The Haven for as long as I have, come to think of it."

"Why don't you leave, then?"

"Because I have nowhere else to go," he says, laughing mirthlessly. "Your departure is disappointing but not heart breaking. Something else that is heart breaking happened today. Life wrote a bittersweet ending for me and then ran out of sugar."

"What?"

He pauses for a while, and we hear the sound of Eden shaking up a cocktail behind us, laughing with the customers at the bar counter. "I have officially ended things with the love of my life," Lucien says flatly.

"Oh wow, I'm so sorry."

"No, don't be. From the looks of it, you did too."

"I don't know what you're –"

"I might look stupid, but I'm actually not. I'm talking about – would you mind terribly if I say her name?"

"I –"

"You're right, I shouldn't. Some names are not meant to be said by others. Well, your girl has a nice air around her. It matches yours. It matches anyone's, actually. Did you know that the air around you has a colour?"

"No I didn't."

"Well, it's invisible for the most part so I don't blame you for being unaware. But if you look closely, under certain lights and angles, it is as clear as day. Everyone's colour is different. It's not distinctive like a typeface so it takes a while to recognise. Fortunately, I have a lot of time on my hands. Donny's looks like sunlight on a lion's mane. Quinn's looks like a burgundy suit saved from a fire. Yours looks like the ocean after a rainstorm."

"What's yours?"

"Mine looks like an army of red flags, like a HDB flat on National Day."

"Technically those are red and white."

"Ah yes, the white is for surrender," he says. "Your girl's air looks like ice cream with rainbow bread."

"It looks like what?"

"Ice cream with rainbow bread. You know the raspberry

ripple, chocolate, durian, coconut, sweet corn and all sorts of other ice cream that the ice cream uncles put between slices of multi-coloured bread? Haven't you ever eaten that before? The air around her looks like that."

We do not say anything more until our cocktails arrive. Lucien's drink, with lychees bobbing in it, is in a tall glass topped by a paper crane. Mine is in a fortune cat tiki cup. I take a sip and cringe slightly. I immediately turn to Eden to apologise for my reaction but she laughs.

"The first sip is meant to be a little sour but there's an underlying sweetness to it. Give it a good stir to bring out its best flavours. But hey, if you don't like it by the third sip, I'll send over a different concoction."

"Thanks Eden, you're the best," Lucien says. "Mine tastes like nectar from the gods."

I take another sip after giving it a stir. I still wince but the sourness is not as strong as it initially was. When I take my third sip, I see what Eden was talking about. There is an unexpected sweetness underlying the sour introduction. It is quite delicious. I see that Eden is watching me closely. I give her a thumbs up and she grins and walks off.

Lucien finishes half of his cocktail by the time she is back behind the bar counter. He turns to me seriously. "Do you know Pope Gregory IX?"

"Not personally, no."

"When he was in power, he decided one day that cats were associated with devil worship and had them slaughtered in outrageous numbers. This was back in the 1200s I believe."

"Are you drunk already, Lucien?"

"On the surface, this seems like just the mass killing of cats, but many would say that the loss of all these felines helped rats spread the Black Death that caused hundreds of millions of people to die."

"Is this your warped version of small talk?"

"My point is, regardless of how historically accurate this story is, it shows that any action we make, however reasonable it seems at the start, could have dire consequences."

"Slaughtering hundreds of cats hardly sounds reasonable."

"Which leads me to my next question. What's the real reason that you're leaving The Haven? Is it because of Donny?"

"No, it's not because of Donny."

"Is it because of what Madam Mischief did with – "

"I don't want to talk about it, Lucien."

"I apologise. We can talk about something else."

Lucien finishes his drink and allows his head to loll on the back of the sofa. The half-light of the bar accentuates the dark circles around his eyes. He looks physically and emotionally exhausted.

"Are you okay?" I ask.

"That is a highly existential question. Ask anyone that at any point of the day and you would get a variety of answers."

"I ask that because you just told me that you broke up with the love of your life."

"I could have meant that in a symbolic sense."

"Did you?"

"No."

Lucien sighs. "This was a self-inflicted wound. To tell you the truth, I was hoping that I'd feel more awful."

"Why would you want to feel more awful?"

"When you argue with someone, there's a weight that the two of you carry together. But the weight is never equally distributed. So I found myself seeking punishment, to be placed in a state of melancholy that I deserved. I stepped in dog poo despite having enough time to side step away from it. I listened to The Perishers with purpose. I walked home from a meeting in the rain, denying myself a cab home. I hope that my efforts helped. I hope that she woke up today feeling lighter."

Our food arrives. Lucien picks up a chicken wing and bites into the steaming flesh, coughing on it. I have a piece of the salted egg yolk popcorn and its familiar yet new flavour surprises my tongue. Lucien tosses back the rest of his drink and orders a Singaporean Old Fashioned.

Almost an hour later and another two cocktails in, Lucien asks me if he can tell me his story. I tell him that it would be my honour. So, with a heavy heart expressed in his trademark monotone voice, he begins.

"Around a year ago, I was dating a young woman named Putri. Her family disproved of the relationship and after a huge quarrel, she came to live with me in The Haven. We were immensely happy together. All we did was laugh loudly, have sex and cook together. She had a beautiful mind. She'd help Donny with decorating The Haven in exchange for living there rent-free. Every blank wall was a canvas to her. Donny and her got along really well. He once told me that if we were to ever get married, he would like to be my best man. The three of us were like a family. It was the happiest time of my life.

"But then one day, something started plaguing my mind and no matter how much I tried to convince myself that I was overthinking, it just would not dissipate. Laughter felt stale on my soul. An orgasm was nothing more than a guilty release.

"Every day was another reminder that I was ruining a once happy family. Because of my place in Putri's life, she would forever be distant from her disapproving parents and sisters. I began to resent myself. I drew away from her and she could not understand why."

Lucien picks up the paper crane that was atop his first

cocktail by its tail and spins it slowly with his thumb and index finger.

"This went on for over a month till I could not take it any longer. So I came up with a plan. I waited till she went out clubbing with her friends, picked the perfect time of the night when she would be tipsy enough to escalate a fight to call her and tell her not to come home. I had packed up all her things and left them outside of The Haven. I told her that my friend had seen her kissing another man."

He shakes his head when he sees the expression on my face. "It was completely untrue, of course. It was nowhere near the truth. But I built up this anger inside of me till it felt like reality. Then eventually, it became a reality that made me lash out at her with every fibre of my being. Every frustration, every heartache, every ounce of self-hatred I had was thrown at this poor woman till she had no voice left to argue back. She had rushed home in a taxi to The Haven, only to find her belongings at the front door waiting for her. I told her that I never wanted to see her again. I could hear her insisting that she had not betrayed me. I knew that she didn't. I knew that I was the one who had betrayed her.

"She only left the next morning. Donny sat on the front steps with Putri till she left. He called her a cab to bring her and her things away. I could hear the sound of the car leave but I stayed in my room. I would not leave it for three days. Food lost its taste without her, water was a necessity but it tasted metallic on my tongue."

"How long ago was this?" I ask.

"This was a year ago," Lucien says conversationally.

"Then why did you say –"

"Today is her wedding day," Lucien says, picking up the paper crane gently, stroking its head as though it were a living thing. "She married a man who loves and cherishes her, and who her parents approved of from the start. He was chasing her when the two of us were together and she found herself in his arms when we broke up. I'm happy for her. You know what? I'm relieved."

I am at a loss for words. My drink is in front of me and though my throat is dry I cannot move. Lucien laughs at the look on my face.

"I know what you want to call me. Go ahead. I guarantee that whatever you say, I've called myself worse."

"I don't deserve to say anything to you. You put her relationship with her family over yours."

"I robbed her of the choice to come to that decision herself. It's not heroic. It's arrogant and selfish. But that's who I am."

"Do you regret what you did?"

"I don't regret what cannot be fixed." He says this while staring down at his feet.

*

On the park bench, one night many years before, Zephyr turned to me. I think she was dressed in her favourite green T-shirt and shorts. She was not smoking that time. She was holding a pack of chips, chomping away as she listened intently to a story that I was telling her. I cannot remember what I was saying, but it was definitely something that I was excited about because I remember her lips curving upwards into a smile when I was done.

She cocked her head at me. "Do you think that you are someone special?" she said.

It came across like a tease, but there was something potent about that moment. The world stopped turning. Opposite the park bench, a pigeon hovered, its wings not fully open for flight but it stayed suspended in mid-air.

"Do you think that you're special?" she repeated, the underlying tenderness even more evident. Then she smiled, positively glowing. "You are. To me."

How I let someone like her go is beyond me. I could blame ignorance but I cannot lie to myself. Even back then I already knew that she was magic.

"Vesuvius has nothing compared to what I'm feeling internally right now."

"Is this what you had in mind?" Donny says to Caroline, referring to The Haven's rooftop set-up.

When Donny agreed to host Caroline's event, she admitted that a part of her was worried about his tendency towards chaos. But that is where she was sorely mistaken. Donny's specialty is not escalation. His specialty is knowing what people want without them saying a word.

After refusing to show Caroline the set-up till the eleventh hour, Donny finally takes her up to the rooftop. Judging by her expression as she enters, it perfectly matches her vision. The space is prepared for an intimate affair, decked with botanical arrangements highlighted by peonies and enveloped by fairy lights to create a firefly filled forest setting. The seating is arranged like a campfire. Circling a small spot-lit stage readied with a microphone are chairs for guests to sit on. At the far end of the rooftop stands a pop-up bar with Lucien shaking up concoctions, his face screwed up with concentration. A basket of animal masks sits by the entrance.

Caroline beams at Donny. "It really is. How did you know that I adore peonies? I'm not the red roses kind of girl."

"At this point, you should only be surprised when I miss my target," Donny winks.

As soon as the sky begins to dim, the guests stream in. Caroline and Donny, who make a great team, greet each by name with warm smiles and welcoming body language. Donny has invited some regulars of The Haven for their interesting backstories. It is apparent that Caroline did not rely entirely on Donny's contacts; she had sent invitations on her own without the use of her Instagram.

"Hey there Brian and Macy," she says to a couple, she in flowing chiffon and he in subtle hand-painted batik. "How was your fifth anniversary celebration? Did you find your perfect romantic place for your staycation?"

A man in boho chic enters. "Hey Arthur, glad to see that you kept the beard you grew from your trip to Tibet. I look forward to hearing more about it later," he says.

"Hello cookie and jam!" she says to the Instagram pair in colour coordinated outfits of different designs. "A reunion of fellow fans of good brunch food. How's your mother doing, jam?"

"These masks are more than a nice touch, Keith," he explains to a bespectacled young man in a Henley T-shirt and leather jacket. "You could call them modern armour."

Then to my surprise, in saunters a man who immediately captures the attention of almost everyone at the rooftop. The gazes stay fixated on his chiselled, handsome features as Isaac approaches Caroline with a gigantic bouquet of red roses in hand. She takes them from him with a wry smile.

Donny suppresses his temptation to laugh as he leans towards me. "Chong owes me $100. I bet him that Isaac would pull off a grand gesture for Caroline within a month of meeting her."

"You think that he's already in love?"

"Nonsense. It's never about love for Isaac, unless it's wanting for himself."

Caroline takes to the stage looking regal under the spotlight. The rooftop of animal faces fall silent waiting for her to speak. She is wearing a mask of a white wolf.

I am holding on to an animal mask of my own – I could not identify with any of the masks in the box so I settled for the face of a cat. It makes me look like one caught in headlights.

"Thank you everyone for accepting my invitation," she says. "Tonight's gathering is a celebration. It's happening not just for you, but also because of you. I am just so happy that you are here."

She's using a different voice tonight as she explains how she wants her guests to share their deepest feelings. It's subtle, hidden under her trademark bubbliness but I notice a tiny shift in cadence adding a reassuring tone. She sounds like someone speaking to kindred spirits reunited after many lost years. It sends a ripple effect across the rooftop. Some were fidgeting in their chairs moments before, self-conscious about sharing their hidden insecurities with a rooftop full of strangers. They're not anymore. They feel like they belong now.

Like everyone else, I am so engrossed in Caroline's aura that I fail to notice Isaac approaching until it is too late. He stands beside me, a lion mask over his face.

"Look at her," he says.

I think we all are, Isaac.

He shakes his head at me in disbelief. "So she likes you, huh? Bro, I have newfound respect for you. You have to tell me your move."

Caroline says something that I did not catch but everyone else bursts out laughing, some breaking into applause. She seems to be cajoling, motivating and appealing in turn, controlling the entire mood of the rooftop.

"Even my best move didn't work. You want to hear it? It's

tough to execute but it works wonders when delivered by the right person. 'I dare you to walk away'."

I turn to him, confused. He laughs.

"That's the line. 'I dare you to walk away'. I swear it works every time. In business or chatting up chicks, I wait for the perfect moment to say that and it never fails. Because I know that they won't. I know the exact moment when I have somcone enraptured and nothing will move him or her away from me. You see I may not be as charming as Donny, who can make anyone trust him from the moment they meet him. But I know I have magnetism. I always get what I want and so of course I assumed that I'd get her too."

I wonder why he is saying all this to me. Then something about the way he speaks catches my attention. I cannot see his expression but his stance and gestures suggest that he is not just talking to me.

"I thought that I had her wrapped around my finger, mistaking artistry for red thread. But her voice, I tell you. That damn voice of hers killed me. Then she gave me this look and smiled and I felt dizzy without even being drunk. But of course I stuck to my guns. Player's got to play. You know what I mean?"

"Yeah, totally," I say, but he doesn't seem to hear me. He is in his own world under a spotlight in front of an invisible audience, gesturing and directing his words at them.

"I used every trick in the book. She was falling for it too. She was giving me all the right signals like playing with her hair, prolonged eye contact, playfully hitting me and so on. So at the perfect moment I pulled her close on the dance floor and said, 'I know that you're having the time of your life with me right now. I dare you to walk away.'"

He shakes his head again, as though still in disbelief. "And holy shit, she actually did. And I found myself watching her for the entire night. I think at points she forgot I was even there. What the hell has she done to me?"

On stage, Caroline ends her introduction and asks for a round of applause to boost everyone's courage. Joining in the applause, Isaac leaves my side to take a seat with the rest of the masked guests.

Caroline is now asking who will speak first. Donny could not have raised his hand any faster. It shoots up in the air, eliciting a burst of laughter from the crowd. At the bar, Lucien shakes his head in mirth. A peacock mask over his features, Donny swaggers to the stage like a gladiator, then poses like Raffles for a long, swelling moment. When the laughter fades, he speaks.

"My name is Donald. It means ruler of the world," he says. "But it is my Dad who has all the power," he continues. "He walks into a room and everything stops. People are on the tips of their toes, ready to bow at any second to claim favour. He used to tell me, 'Boy, it is not important to be someone who people love. It is important to be someone who people respect.' And I thought that sounded so lonely."

Even when Donny bears his soul, his mannerisms are theatrical. The way that he gesticulates, draws the laughter, breaks for pauses, paces on stage and holds himself, all incline towards the dramatic.

I am the only one who notices the middle-aged man who has made his way to the rooftop, standing by the entrance.

I recognise him right away. He's Quinn's father. He still looks timid and sweaty but is no longer hesitant. His fists are clenched and his steady gaze is focused on Quinn.

She finally sees him through her lens and freezes, the camera grasped more tightly in hand. She lowers the camera. No one notices this interaction – everyone is gazing up at Donny, spellbound.

Quinn rushes over to her father. She does not seem to notice me as she brushes past. She takes his arm and pulls him into the stairwell.

I can just faintly make out their words, snatches of the conversation.

"That still doesn't explain why you're here," she says in response to something he said.

His answer is lost to me.

"I feel safe here – more than I've ever felt back in that house of yours," she says, raising her voice at him.

He says something about "your mother's grave."

Quinn replies, "Yes I have. Just not with you. Can't you just leave me be?" Her voice is loud with anger.

"I can't. You're my daughter," he retorts.

"I'm my mother's daughter, not yours. And don't expect me to go back to that house now that my secret keeper is gone."

Then I hear footsteps as Quinn bundles her father down the stairs.

Cue roaring applause. Donny is ending his speech.

"I will never, for as long as I live, share my father's ideology of power. I refuse to. I don't want to be the reason why a room goes still. I want to make people feel alive. My name is Donald. Remember me. It means ruler of the world."

Donny lifts the microphone like how Liberty holds her torch. His head is tilted to the sky. He holds this pose for seconds, then slowly lowers the mic with outstretched arm, waiting for someone to take it from him.

If someone chose this moment to walk in, we would look like a cult. I look around at the sea of animal faces. A young woman in an elephant mask rises from her seat and takes the microphone from Donny. In that moment, she is braver than I have ever been in my entire life. Donny bows to her in acknowledgment, as though asking her for a dance. She takes her place on the stage.

She replaces his thundering voice with silence. First, she just stands there, on her tiptoes, as though peering over the edge of a skyscraper. Then she is back on her heels, swaying gently like a breeze is rocking her. There is not a sound from the others on the rooftop, not even a cough or a stifled sneeze. When she finally speaks, her voice shakes. She is a victim of sexual abuse from someone who she trusted more than anyone.

When the young woman finishes, two girls in bird masks go forward and hug her.

Then, in turn, people in the circle get up on stage to share their stories. Not all of them are sad. Some are hilarious, others thoughtful. After one speaker, Isaac gets up from his seat and moves forward. He walks towards the stage with quick determined steps but passes it, continues to the end of the space and exits the rooftop.

I find Donny next to me now. I feel his hand on my back as he pushes me forward. I consider bolting for the door. He claps his hands enthusiastically and everyone else joins in.

My knees shake as I stumble to the centre of the rooftop and get up on stage. I feel like I am moving in slow motion. It is brighter up here than it looked from where I was. I can feel myself breathing hard behind my mask. It is less than two feet above the ground but it feels like I am walking on a tightrope on the edge of the world. The crowd around me gazes up expectantly, from the hippo to the fox, to the deer to the bullfrog, to my friends the peacock and the white wolf who gives me a thumbs up.

My face is like a furnace behind the mask. The more I stand in the silence, the harder it is to ignore.

I close my eyes for a quick second to stop sweat from getting into my eyes. When I do, I find myself back in my old childhood bedroom. I instantly recognise the blue-coloured plaster on the walls and the painting of an apple tree above my study desk. I'm dressed in my Tintin pyjamas, sitting on the edge of my bed, knees tucked tightly to my chest. On the other end of the room is my father, sitting in a chair shaped like a teddy bear.

It should be a comical sight but he still manages to look menacing, staring at me with his unblinking, piercing gaze. When he finally speaks, he barely moves a muscle on his face. His voice is no higher than a whisper.

"Look at you, boy," he says. After all these years, he still manages to send a chill down my spine. "So lost in your head. Playing hide and seek even though no one's looking for you."

I can feel his power from over here. The room seems to tremor in response to every word he says. My father and I make eye contact for a quick second and I immediately shift my gaze to the polka dotted carpet in the centre of the floor.

He shakes his head in disgust at this act of submission. "Stop looking down. It's a coward's way out of conflict. Contrary to what your mother believes, the world is not entitled to give you anything. You are not special. If you're not moving, you're waiting. You can't keep hiding in the silence like it's –"

For the life of me I cannot explain what I do next. I reach for the bottom of my mask and remove it. I breathe in the fresh air deeply.

The crowd takes this as a dramatic prelude to my monologue. Some cheer, others woot. Caroline lets out a loud whistle.

I look up to lock eyes with my father from across the room. I snatch the words out of his throat and he goes quiet. The cold fury on his face gives way to surprise, as he looks at me, stunned. I smile. Listen closely, Dad.

"I'm not interesting," I say.

Those words seem to pique everyone's interest. "Every one

of you deserves applause, the spotlight. I wish that you knew. And I hope that you now do."

Every time I stop talking, the rooftop gets swallowed by silence. And the silence is entirely my burden to dictate and to fill as the crowd waits to be engaged and entertained. I am already exhausted.

I see Caroline cock her head at me. Lucien has left the pop-up bar counter to stand next to her and Donny. I soldier on.

"I am a magician. I make the good things in my life disappear. Unlike most tricks, it's something that I can repeat endlessly without knowing how the magic works. I don't have an extensive list of people whom I can call in the middle of the night when the world gets too heavy. All I have is a birthday card written in brilliant scrawl every year without fail reminding me that I am one of the lucky ones. Abracadabra. It doesn't disappear. Hocus Pocus! It remains there. I have a million words in my arsenal to make good things go away but this is the one thing that stays."

My hands are shaking, more theatrical than I realise, I silently wish that someone in the crowd would remove her mask and reveal Zephyr, smiling at me, telling me that everything would be okay. But I have not earned myself such a brilliant ending.

"I hurt the person that I care about the most in the world. I have... dawning realisations about my best friend. I finally recognise my soulmate. I am at the cliché of a romcom where the protagonist should run through the airport to stop the girl he loves from boarding a plane. But it's too late. People say that it's never too late, but it really is for me. I guess that's what I deserve for being so caught up in my own head."

The spotlight seems brighter than it was before as I look up at it and immediately regret my action. When I look down at my audience, they are drenched with spots. In this golden haze, I imagine Zephyr here.

"I'm nothing special, but perhaps that's okay. I don't chase approval because in my heart, I know something that no one can quantify. My world is something subjective, unrecognisable to everyone but myself. My world is different from yours, as is yours from everyone else's. Your world could be a place, an objective, or even a person. My world is something that I hold close. Closer than close, and all you need to know is that I shall forever fight through heaven and hell to protect it."

I expect a piercing silence when I finish, but the quiet that I succumb to is quite different. It feels like an embrace. Donny rises to his feet, removing his mask and clapping loudly and rhythmically. He is looking at me with an expression that I have never seen before. Lucien and Caroline, who have also removed their masks, beam up at me. Caroline's eyes look watery. Perhaps it is a trick of the lights. The others on the rooftop join in the applause. It is the most theatrical form of validation that I have ever experienced in my life and I give a bow.

I feel recognised.

"Wish that I would've stayed too."

When the event ends, Caroline, Lucien and I stay on the rooftop as the hired help clears up. Donny excuses Quinn and himself, saying that they are going downstairs for a chat. We open up a bottle of red wine. It feels nice, drinking with friends. When we laugh, it seems to fill up the entire roof.

Lucien is smiling genuinely for the first time in a while as he shares with Caroline about the air that surrounds her. She laughs when he tells her that it looks like a red gypsy dress in a sea of grey T-shirts.

I excuse myself for a toilet break and head to my room. When I pass Donny's bedroom, the door is ajar. Through the crack I can see him with Quinn. She is crying, her face in her hands. It is rude to eavesdrop but this is as much as I hear.

"Don't be like that. You know that you're always welcome here. But maybe it's best that you go home," Donny says, his voice more tender than I have ever heard.

"I thought that this was home," Quinn says, choking through sobs.

"This is The Haven. It's not home. That's the point, Quinn."

I return to Lucien and Caroline. Soon, Donny and Quinn rejoin us on the rooftop. Quinn's eyes are a little puffy but she quickly switches back to her flirtatious, cheeky self as

219

though what I just witnessed never happened. A consummate professional, Donny acts the same.

Caroline tells me that I am more charismatic than I realise. She says that my speech was one of the standouts of the evening. I am certain that she is just being polite by saying so, but I appreciate the sentiment.

"What are your plans for the weekend, Melbourne boy?" she says.

I tell her that perhaps I will stay up all night, make myself some tea and put on an Al Green album and watch the sunrise.

"I think I got arthritis from listening to that," Donny remarks.

"Oh hush," Caroline says, slapping him playfully on the arm. "I think that it sounds like a brilliant morning. There's nothing more comforting in this world than an old soul."

Quinn starts to whistle "Let's Stay Together" by Al Green. Following her lead, Donny taps his foot and slaps his palms on his thighs to create rhythm. Caroline and Lucien harmonise the tune and when the four of them are finished with the song, I clap loudly.

"That's one of his greatest songs," I say.

"I wish we recorded that," Caroline says. "Someone once told me that it was their mother's favourite song."

"That would be me," Quinn says.

"Oh yes! I remember," Caroline says. "Maybe we could do it again and video it for her."

"She's passed away."

"I'm so sorry, I didn't –"

"It's fine," Quinn says. She picks up her phone and shows Caroline her wallpaper. "This is Mama Mischief."

"She's beautiful," Caroline says. "Were the two of you close?"

Donny opens his mouth to speak in an attempt to change the subject, but Quinn places a hand on his thigh and he relaxes. "She was the only thing that made our bungalow feel like a home. She was my best friend."

Quinn looks surprised by her own admission but something about Caroline's gaze makes her continue. "I used to have my slumber parties sans slumber at home but got tired of my father cooking breakfast for my 'friends' and asking how we met. The girl and I would have to concoct stories together. We met at school. We're working on a project and have an early shoot tomorrow. It was exhausting. So when Donny offered me solace, I took it. And life's been amazing ever since."

He smiles warmly at her. "Life's been more amazing because of you too," he says. Quinn smiles back.

"You're a gentleman and a pirate, Donny," says Caroline. "You should be proud of how The Haven both saves and entertains everyone who enters it."

"I won't say everyone," Donny replies, refilling my wine glass then everyone else's. For a second I think that he's referring to me. But then he pauses before pouring wine into Caroline's glass.

"Do you mean me?" she says, surprised.

"Yes I do."

"Silly boy, I'm having the time of my life. All that you've done for me –"

"– Isn't enough," Donny interrupts. I recognise that look. He's doing that thing he always does. He has held back on probing for far too long and can no longer be courteous. "You haven't posted on Instagram for many months now."

Caroline's lips tighten. Quinn stops mid-inhale of her vape as Lucien's look shifts between Caroline and Donny.

"And honestly, I don't need to know the reason. But it's clear that you miss it. You miss it so much that you can't even bear to speak about it yet something holds you back. I know it's not my place to say this, but whatever it is, please don't let it win. Nothing should stop you from doing what you love."

Caroline sips wine thoughtfully. "I do miss it," she says after a while.

Donny seems to know exactly what she has been through, and chooses not to probe further. It is their secret. At least he makes it seem that way.

"Don't let go of what helps you breathe easier," he says. As always, his voice emanates charisma. "Whatever you lost, or associated to loss on that incredible platform of yours, is not forever. You don't need to search for new joys like hosting events and putting chauvinists in their place if you're already lucky enough to have something. This old joy may sting once in a while, but who needs good all the time? It's like being beaten over the head repeatedly with a rainbow. It's worth it. You deserve to love what you love. So lean on what leans on you."

Caroline flushes, embarrassed as though Donny is flipping through her diary and reading the contents out loud.

When she recovers, she asks, "What world did you come from to make you who you are, Donny Liang?"

He smiles at her. "I'm from here," is his reply. "Worlds away from a chilli sauce empire."

*

After we finish the wine, we head to the front of The Haven for a parting cigarette. Donny and Quinn join Caroline for one. I stand there with them, used to the smell of second-hand smoke. After they are done, Lucien hugs Caroline goodbye and she kisses him on the cheek. He looks over the moon. Quinn wraps her arms around Donny and Lucien's waists ready to head inside. They wait for me to follow suit but I tell them to go ahead.

It is nearing daybreak, and the clouds are parting to make way for sunlight. Caroline and I are now alone outside of The Haven. She smiles at me cheekily. "Is this the part of the story where you ravage me in the middle of the empty street?" she says.

"You won't be drowning any more sharks tonight, Caroline."

She laughs, shaking her head. "Ah, Isaac. I'm impressed that he managed to fit his humongous head through The Haven's rooftop door."

She takes a long, thankful look at The Haven.

"Donny was right though," she says. "Hosting a party just didn't feel the same as doing Instagram Live. What do you think?"

"What do *you* think?" I say.

She lifts her head to the dawn and lets out a gentle breath. "I guess I should stop fighting it, huh?"

Caroline does not move a muscle but in a split-second she changes completely. It is something I have never witnessed in anyone before. Something powerful and beautiful emanates from her face as she stares into the distance. "Hello everyone, it's been a while."

Then she changes the inflexion of her words.

She says the words in the same sequence one more time, but it sounds completely different from before. It feels like an embrace from a best friend and I find myself moved.

She turns to me. "Which one?"

"The third one," I choose. "Are you about to do what I think you're about to do?"

"I suppose I am, magic man." Caroline accesses Instagram on her phone. She scrolls through her profile's images, and smiling to herself she turns on Instagram Live. Nothing happens for a moment, and then, one by one, her audience logs in. Before I know it, there are over a hundred people watching Caroline standing alone in the middle of an empty street in the morning light.

'You're back!' someone comments.

'Oh my god, *morethanfourleafclover* has returned! Where did you go?' another says.

'How have you been? Wow, it has been ages!' yet another types.

A long stream of comments and hearts float up her screen as Caroline begins.

"Hello everyone, it's been a while."

Her voice carries so much ache.

"I want to explain my absence. I've been hiding from it but I'm ready to share it with each of you. Something terrible happened six months ago. My boyfriend passed away. He was and will forever be the love of my life and everything about my Instagram profile made me think of him. The places that we used to go together, the food we used to eat, the memories that we shared. It was too much to bear for the longest time, even now."

Comments stream in at increased velocity. "Thank you for all your heartfelt comments. You don't know how grateful I am. I ask for your forgiveness and your patience. I won't be on here as often as before, and the photographs will definitely not look as amazing as they used to. Michael, my Houdini, was the one who took all the pictures you liked. From this moment on, it's entirely up to me and I don't want to just tell you about my day or shout out for the brands I'm wearing and the cafes I'm eating at. I want to hear from every single one of you. I want you to tell me about your joys, triumphs and tragedies. I want to be here for you as you have always been for me. I have missed every single one of you. I promise that I'll see you soon and that I will get better."

She turns off Instagram Live and reaches into her purse for a cigarette and tries to light up. Her hand is shaking hard. I take the lighter and light the cigarette for her.

She lets out a mist of smoke that covers her flushed cheeks. Then she speaks brightly, in the voice that I recognise she promised to save for me. "How was that? Have you fallen in love with me yet?"

I cannot help but chuckle and she responds warmly. "Look at that, I made you laugh. Maybe I'm magic too."

She pecks me on the cheek and walks to her car. She gets in, waves goodbye and I am alone.

I check the time. It is almost 7 am but I am nowhere near close to being tired. In fact, I have never felt more awake in my life. I walk to the main road and flag a taxi almost without realising it and get in. The cab driver asks me where I would like to go.

"I'd like to go back to the start," I say.

The driver turns around to face me with a weary expression. "Bro, if you're drunk, I have plastic bags in the back. But I need the address of the place you want to go to."

I tell him that I want to go to the airport.

When we arrive, the sky brims with new light. Grey with scattered stars makes way for bluish crimson. I exit the car and walk through the sliding doors to the departure hall and stand in front of the digital flight schedule. I look up at the yellow words flashing on the large black screen. I wonder if there is someplace that I could take off to, even for just a day, even for the most fleeting of moments. Countries upon countries glow before my eyes enticingly. I could go anywhere. I could even return to Melbourne if I wanted to.

One moment I am standing in front of the digital flight board, the next moment I am in the back of another taxi. I tell the cab driver to take me back to my old family flat. He talks during the entire ride, trying to jumpstart a conversation but I remain disengaged. I'm saving my words for someone else. Two people, in fact.

I get out of the taxi and head upstairs to my family's apartment. The key is still in my wallet. I take it out at the door, unlock it and walk in.

I feel disconnect immediately. There is little trace of home in this place.

I pull my phone out of my pocket and punch a familiar number. It rings while I feel my breath coming out in shudders. When the person on the other end of the line picks up, I inexplicably inhale deeply.

"Hello, is this who I think this is?" she says. I must have caught her in the middle of brunch because there is the sound of cutlery on plates and people talking loudly in the background.

I exhale and say, "Hey Andrea. It's me."

"Are you alright? Where are you now?"

"I'm in Singapore."

"Why are you – wait, hang on."

There is a sound of a door shutting and then silence. She must have walked out of the café and while doing so, had time to gather her thoughts and collect her venom.

"You went to Singapore to find your precious Zephyr, didn't you?"

"Look, if I caught you at a bad time –"

"Answer the damn question."

"I came to Singapore to clear my head."

"Is that why you're calling? You want to yell at me for what I did?"

"No, I don't want to yell at you. I just want to know why you did it."

226

There is a pause on the other end of the line. I hear her fumbling in her pocket and then with a clicking sound, she inhales deeply and exhales. It sounds like a sigh.

"I thought you said that you were going to quit smoking," I say.

"Oh, shut up. You're being oddly confrontational. Are you drunk?"

"No I'm not."

"Are you dating Zephyr now?"

Andrea still says Zephyr's name as though she is some kind of disease-carrying insect.

"Is that why you did it?" I ask.

Andrea snorts loudly. "Seriously, what is this? Are you trying to get me to apologise? Do you want me to beg?"

"No, I just want to know if I owe you an apology."

"...What did you just say? You really must be drunk."

"I want to know why you cheated on me, because if it is in any way my fault, I'd like to apologise."

"This isn't funny. If I'm on loudspeaker right now and your friends are in the background just –"

"I'm alone, Andrea. And I'm being serious."

She is quiet for so long that I almost wonder if she hung up. But then she finally speaks and her voice sounds shaky.

"*Here's your chance to run.*"

That's what she used to say to me every single time she introduced me to a skeleton in her closet. Andrea was a woman with scars and stories. On our first date she told me that she had recently gotten out of an abusive relationship. She showed me the bruises on her stomach and back. Before our first kiss, she said to me for the first time – "here's your chance to run."

I didn't. On our fourth date, she told me that she used to cut herself. She got naked and showed me her scars. Before

227

we had sex she said, "Here's your chance to run." I didn't again.

"I used to think that you never judged me because you loved me," Andrea says. "But I realised that it was because you just didn't care enough about me."

"That's not true – "

"You loved Zephyr so much. I could feel it. My parents could feel it, that night when you got drunk over dinner. In my house, drinking my dad's expensive whiskey, while eating the food that I cooked and prepared and spent weeks to perfect."

"I already know that I – "

"I'm to blame, really. I opened up the can of worms. When we first started dating, I realised that alcohol was our means of communication. One drink and you'd start to loosen up, crack a smile here and there. Two drinks in and you'd start displaying your wit. I didn't realise at first how funny and secretly snarky you were. Three drinks in and you'd gradually display affection. It was my mistake for pushing you beyond that. Four drinks in and you'd talk about Zephyr."

After that fateful dinner with Andrea's parents, where I apparently talked about Zephyr for almost an hour straight, Andrea treated me differently. I did not realise how hurt she was till this moment.

"You love her so much," she says. "And my heart and pride couldn't handle it. I tried to reassure myself that you loved me but deep down I knew that I could never mean more to you than she did."

"So that's why you cheated on me?"

"I didn't have the heart to. At first, anyway. It started as an obsession. I used to drive my friends crazy from talking about you for every minute of every day. I had all these theories and I was analysing your every gesture, your every word, to try and figure you out. To try and quantify how much I meant to you. Then when everyone got fed up with my incessant whining, I decided to take things into my own hands. It started out small. Remember how I used to call you babe-o?"

"I remember."

"I started giving your pet name to other guys. Colleagues, our mutual friends, men who would hit on me – I'd call them that in front of you. No reaction. Not even a twitch of jealousy. So I went further. I'd invite other men along for our lunch dates. I'd exclude you from our inside jokes. I'd hold men by the arm, kiss them on the cheek in front of you. Nothing. You didn't even care."

Her voice sounds like it is on the verge of breaking. I think that she has started to cry. "My ex-boyfriend used to beat me up. You've seen the scars, you'd know. He made me feel like the ugliest person on the planet. But at least it was something. You made me feel like nothing. I was sick of complaining about you. So tired and exhausted of crying about you, of being in love with someone who felt nothing for me. So I did something awful. I just needed to know. I had sex with Jason because I knew that you'd come into the office. You told me you had work to do that day. I knew you'd come to the office and walk in on us. When you did, I looked you in the eye. And I didn't see sadness. I didn't see betrayal. I didn't even see anger. It was just shock and nothing else. It killed me. I ruined myself for you."

Then I hear it. She breaks, anguished sobs ringing out from the other end of the receiver.

"Andrea," I say but she keeps crying. "Andrea," I repeat. "I'm sorry for how I made you feel. You were good to me and I was an awful, emotionally distant boyfriend. I should have never pushed you to this extent and I didn't know that I made you feel this way."

She is silent for a long time except for the sound of heavy breathing.

"Andrea, I'm sorry," I say again.

There finally comes a dry laugh from her. "You almost sound sincere, you soulless freak," she says. "Don't pretend to care about me. You never did and at this moment, I can tell that you still don't."

I don't know what else to say.

"Now's your chance to run," she says before hanging up on me.

*

After possibly the worst phone call in the history of the universe, I call up another familiar Melbourne number. My mother picks up almost instantaneously. She must be in the office. There is the sound of typing keyboards, people chattering and telephones ringing in the background.

"Hello, my sun and moon," she says. "What perfect timing, you called me just as I was about to head out for lunch. Have you eaten breakfast yet? You always skip breakfast, you know, it's not good for you. At least have a slice of toast with peanut butter or *kaya* – hey, remember when I used to call Gary's ex-wife Vegemite because they both make me want to vomit? Yesterday I accidentally ate Gary's breakfast sandwich instead of mine, and surprise surprise, it's actually not bad. After all these years of living with an *ang mo*, I finally see why they – oh actually, speaking of *ang mo*, can I put you on loudspeaker? My colleagues Beatrice and Paul keep asking about you. They haven't seen or heard from you since that time you brought me a spare change of clothes when I accidentally spilled coffee on myself. Do you remember that? Anyway, say hello to them, okay? Then as sincerely, impassionedly as possible, declare how much I – "

"I called to tell you something, Mom," I interrupt her.

After an unbelievably long silence, she says, "I'm listening."

"I've decided to not go back to Melbourne."

"I see –"

Before she has the chance to say anything else, I cut in. "But it's not for the reason you think, Mom. I'm standing my ground because I'm tired of hiding at the first sign of conflict. I remember taking comfort in silence when I was a kid, watching you and Dad treat words as weapons."

"Hey, no, it's not your –"

"I know what you're going to say. That's not why I'm telling you this. I just want you to know that from now on I'm not going to hold on to all these things I'm afraid of expressing anymore."

There is a pause before she says, "I hear you."

Then there is a light chuckle over the receiver. "Well, then. Will you be coming back to pack your things and kiss your Mom goodbye?"

"Yes, in due time. But there are things here that I need to take care of and I don't plan on leaving till I've settled them all."

"Good boy. It took you long enough. I hope you realise now how horrible you've been treating that special soul."

"Don't worry, I'm going to apologise to Zephyr as soon as I can. Out of all the things I have to do, it's the top priority."

Then my mother speaks with laughter in her voice. "I was talking about you, kid."

I hang up the phone and go from room to room taking a proper look around my old home. I come face-to-face with a cold kitchen, unplugged television, forgotten books and a dead plant in the living room quietly gathering dust.

Then I notice a note near the front door. I pick it up and

immediately recognise Zephyr's handwriting.

I wish you stayed. Not for me, for anything. Anything at all. I just wish that you stayed.

"X marks the spot."

"This feels so abrupt, we don't even have a photo together," Quinn says, crestfallen.

When I return to The Haven, I tell my housemates that I will be packing up my things and leaving immediately. They are hanging out together in the living room, helping Donny decide his wardrobe for his upcoming client meeting in Indonesia. As expected, almost everything he picked out has a floral element to it. Their laughter dies down as soon as I tell them my decision.

"Are you sure you want to do this?" Lucien says.

I nod. "I really am. I'm thankful for everything you've all done for me. But I have to move forward."

Lucien and Quinn look at each other, and then back at me, dumbfounded. It is as though the comprehension of the English language has suddenly escaped them. Finally, Donny breaks the silence.

"Thanks for allowing us a goodbye," he says. "Maybe my read's off for once, but you seem like someone who'd rather pack his luggage in the middle of the night and leave without a word."

"Your read's never off," I respond.

Donny forces a laugh as I make my way up the stairs to

pack. It is a task that does not take long and within a couple of minutes I am almost done. I notice Lucien watching me from the doorway gloomily. He has a box of cereal that he hands to me.

"Something to remember us by," he says with a sad smile.

"Thank you."

"What time is your flight?" Lucien asks. "If you don't mind, we'd like to send you off at the airport. Have one last hurrah before you leave."

"I'm not going back to Melbourne."

"Oh. Wait, then where – "

"I'm moving back to our old family flat," I tell him. I pack his box of cereal with the rest of my things and zip up my luggage. I rise to my feet and take one last look around the room to make sure that I have not left anything behind. When I am done, I turn to Lucien. He has a genuine smile on his face.

"I'm proud of you," he says.

"Why?"

"Because you're not running away. You're moving forward. It's brave. It's braver than I've dared to be for the past year. I hope that you get everything that you want."

"Well, you could move forward too," I say. A thought occurs to me and as I say it, I wonder why it did not cross my mind sooner. "Why don't you move in with me?"

He looks surprised, turning around to make sure that there is no one behind him. Then he turns back to me, pointing at himself. I nod. He grins nervously. "I'll let you pretend that you didn't say that," he says.

"My dad's gone and my mom's living with her boyfriend in Melbourne. I have a room to spare so you can stay with me as long as you like. Who knows, maybe we could start our own marketing agency."

"Why would you want that? I have more red flags than a –"

"You've said that before, Lucien. It's not a good enough quote to turn into a catchphrase."

Lucien looks suddenly scared, his eyes shifting around nervously as though I just invited him to go skydiving without a parachute. "Why would you want that?" he asks once more.

The longer I spend in this moment the happier I am about my decision. "Because I recognise you," I say, and his face lights up with dawning realisation. "We're introverts from the same typeface. Who won't want that? Besides, I need a cook."

When we tell Donny later, he does not appear the least bit surprised. In fact, neither does Quinn, as she wearily slaps a $50 note into Donny's open palm. Donny smiles broadly as he pulls his housemate of the past year into a tight hug.

"Thanks for letting me have a place in your home, Donny," Lucien says in a muffled voice, his face buried in Donny's shoulder.

"You were a part of The Haven, Lucy," Donny grins. "You always will be. Now let's stop being mushy like baby food so you can get packing."

As Lucien heads upstairs to pack, Donny's expression slips. He makes his way over to the graffiti-stained piano in the living room and sits. He lifts the lid and begins to play. I didn't know that Donny could play the piano. He plays a beautiful melody, one that Quinn recognises. She makes her way across the room and sits down beside him.

She begins to play alongside Donny, he taking the base notes and she the melody. Soon, the composition is no longer someone else's, but one that they created together.

When they finish, I applaud but neither of them appears to hear me. They are in their own elaborate, quiet and large world. Donny smiles at the woman seated next to him.

"I don't want you to leave," he says. "Please don't leave."

It looks as though it took a great deal for him to say that, and Quinn recognises it. She beams back at him. "I wasn't planning to, my friend."

When Lucien has his bags packed, Donny and Quinn help us carry our luggage and boxes of belongings to the front of The Haven.

"Will you promise to visit regularly?" Donny says to Lucien. "I must say I'm going to miss your cooking almost as much as your company."

"Of course. I'll make *bak kuh teh* the next time that I'm here."

"Herbal or peppery?"

"I'll do both. I've also been experimenting with a recipe of dry *bak kuh teh* recommended by my Malaysian friend."

"I can't wait."

Donny turns his attention to me. I extend an arm out to him but he goes in for a hug, pulling me in till my palm rests awkwardly on his stomach. He eventually pulls away but still holds on to my shoulders.

"I have to say, I was hoping that you'd stay longer," he says.

"Why's that?"

Donny looks confused by my question. "Because we're friends," he says. Then he grins, just like how he used to back when we were teenagers, playing Playstation on his couch. "Do you still remember the first time that we talked to each other?"

"I do. You sat down next to me during lunch."

"Do you know why I did that?"

"I don't."

"And you never wondered why?"

"I presume that you thought that I needed fixing."

Donny laughs and shakes his head. "It's not as simple as

that. I wanted to impress you."

"You impress me daily, Donny."

"Not in the way that I'm used to," he says. "Since I was a teen, I fed off being an antidote, a necessity. Then you showed up, completely self-assured. I knew that there was something wanting in you but I just could not figure it out. You were always by your lonesome, never participating in activities and for all these years I wanted to know your secret. Then at the party I saw you with Zephyr and finally I knew. Why you didn't need anyone back in school, or craved for validation from people around you like myself. Why all my efforts to help you find connection in this space failed miserably. You already have safe haven of your own."

As I expected him to, Donny cuffs me on the shoulder. "Can I at least convince you to stay for one drink?" he says.

I apologise. "There's something that I need to do."

He pretends to look offended, gesturing to The Haven. "More important than this?"

I cannot help but smile. "Yes, it is. It's more important than anything."

Donny looks at me as though I am stepping into a spacecraft aimed at a far-away universe. "Lucky you," he says with a smile.

Later on as Lucien and I drive off in a taxi, my new housemate sticks his head out the window, watching his home of the past year fade into the distance. I cannot help but smile at the look on his face.

"How are you feeling?" I ask him.

He is grinning from ear to ear, still waving goodbye to The Haven. "Like I'm on top of the food chain," he says.

*

Sometimes I feel like I was born in the wrong universe. In an alternate dimension I am a sea captain, steering my ship through a terrible storm. I am soaked, drenched from head to toe. If that is not dramatic enough, I am fending off a gang of pirates trying to commandeer the ship. They are threatening beasts with magnificent beards and gold teeth, and some of them even have hooks for hands. They snarl and jeer at me from their ship with black sails as I power on through against the current.

They dare me to capsize. They tell me that I am about to go down with my ship. So I start to sing. I have no battle cry. What I have in my arsenal is a melody that I created in my head. The song has no lyrics, so I make them up as I go along. This makes the pirates confused. It makes them hate me even more. The rain is positively wailing, the waters choppy and dark, and the pirates are dangerously close to taking control of my ship. But I enjoy it. I revel in it, knowing full well that I will not drown because I am the captain. In this chaos, I find myself in a state of infinite calm.

I reach the park bench and sit down in the centre of the universe. I like it in here. It feels like home. I take out my phone and speed dial that familiar number. One ring and there is no answer. Two rings – that is no cause for concern. Three rings is the average but no one picks up. We are now six rings in, and just as I start to wonder if I have lost my opportunity for salvation for good, my call is answered. I should have been less doubting. She always does.

"Hey electric eel," she says, sounding more distant than usual.

"Hey, Zephyr," I say. "It's me. I'm at our sanctuary. I'd like to talk."

"I'm not home at the moment."

"It's alright, I can wait."

"I don't know how long I'll be. I'm at a client's function."

"Take your time. Take all night. Stay over, wake up the next morning for breakfast and a coffee then come. I'll still be here. Take seven years. Take longer. I'll wait forever if I have to. I have all the time in the world."

"You mean more to me than you could even imagine."

Zephyr shows up within half an hour. I see her walk over cautiously, as though to make sure that I am not a mirage.

There is that familiar scent of passionfruit as she joins me on our park bench. Zephyr sets down a plastic bag of items that she takes out one by one. She first pulls out three canned drinks: Milo, chrysanthemum tea and Sprite. I already know that one will be used as an ashtray. Next she pulls out three transparent bags of snacks tied up with rubber bands. They are iced gem biscuits, wheel crackers and butterfly crackers. Finally she takes out a new packet of cigarettes and a lighter and lays them all out between us.

"Which one do you want?" Zephyr says, gesturing to the three canned drinks. I point to the chrysanthemum tea and she nods, taking the Milo and cracking it open. "I got these from Keng Hong Store. Do you still remember it?" she says after taking a gigantic gulp.

"Yes I do," I say. Keng Hong Store is a provision shop just around the corner of our HDB blocks. At the shopfront there are giant golden tins that contain a variety of biscuits and snacks. "I remember skipping recess in primary school just so I could use my lunch money to buy snacks there."

"Yeah, the store uncle still remembers me from when I was

a little girl. Every time I buy smokes from him he gives me this disappointed fatherly look. He keeps my secret though. My mom buys bread from him all the time and he never says a word."

Zephyr taps the cigarette pack and I count silently with her. She always slaps her packs against her palm exactly eight times. I asked her once why she does it but she could not give me a logical explanation.

She now draws a cigarette from the fresh pack and lights it up. She inhales slowly.

When I kissed Zephyr, the world went quiet. I have replayed that moment in my mind countless times after, and cannot bring myself to regret it. For once in my life, I dared to take control of the moment with my lips pressed against hers. Regardless of whatever transpired after, it was that moment of pure bliss that made it all worth it. I kissed her and the world went quiet. Even if it was for the most fleeting of moments.

"So what do you want to talk about?" she says. She is sketching her cigarette in the sky like a paintbrush, making a pattern with the fumes.

"Everything," I say. "How have you been?"

"Busy. The fellas at Donny's party have been amazing leads. I might get my bonus early this year because of Donny. I almost feel bad about calling him a human hot air balloon."

I laugh. Zephyr takes another big gulp from her can of Milo before setting it down on the park bench. She flicks her cigarette ash into it and peers at me, her head cocked to a side. "You look like you just returned from an adventure," she says after a while. "What have you been up to?"

"I've moved out of The Haven."

Her lips twitch. It is the first time that she shows a semblance of a smile since sitting down. "It was just a matter of time.

That place really didn't suit you, Will."

"I also had closure with Andrea."

"Your ex who cheated on you? After escaping that venomous creature you actively turned back around? Were you trying to turn into stone?"

"And I finally ate *ice kachang*."

"It's about time! Did you try it with – "

"*Attap chee*, jelly and red bean? Yes I did. And everything else."

"Kehehe. What else did the electric eel get up to?"

"Brace yourself. I made a speech in front of a room full of people."

"My goodness, look at you. You are full of surprises these days." She takes one final drag of her cigarette before tossing it into the Milo can and continues, "This just about tops your asking me if I was engaged to Ashley!"

"Wow, you just refuse to let that slide."

She giggles and I join in. It feels like a while since we laughed together. The few times that I find myself laughing out loud, my body rocking back and forth like a child, I notice Zephyr follow my direction like I am something magnetic. She leans in as I do, and when I fall to the other side she tilts with me.

As our laughter dies down, she pulls out another cigarette and places it between her lips, looking considerably happier now.

"I suppose belated congratulations are in order," I say, breaking the silence. Zephyr stops in the motion of lighting up. "How did the two of you meet?"

"I thought you brought me here tonight to talk about us."

"That can wait. I'd like to talk about you."

She looks at me curiously. I take the lighter from her hands and use my thumb to roll the metal cog till a flame is ignited. Keeping her eyes on me, she leans in to accept the light before drawing breath and exhaling a stream of smoke.

"It's a long story, Will."

I pick up one of the transparent bags of snacks and untie the rubber band. "I don't have anywhere else to be," I say and her face softens. Now assured, she leans back and tells her story.

"His name is Sebastian," she says, as I open her bag of butterfly crackers. "We met at a whiskey launch that my company organised. We had hired a hot chick who played two pianos at the same time and I remember he was the only man in the crowd who didn't have his eyes glued to her. Instead, I noticed that he kept looking in my direction. Later, he walked up and told me that the only attraction he enjoyed the entire night was what he felt towards me."

"Smooth," I say.

"Smooth has never been my type. But he asked for my phone number and I gave it to him. We had dinner together a couple of nights after."

"I thought you didn't like giving your number to strangers."

Zephyr quickly looks down at her feet, as though she had dropped something. "Yeah, that changed after you left," she says.

She says this without a hint of malice but I wince all the same. She looks up, not hiding behind a bright smile or a kooky look like she always does. For the first time ever she willingly shows me her pain and it is heart-wrenching for me. "You really hurt me when you left without a goodbye," she says. "I thought that we meant the world to each other. A safe space, you know? And I couldn't understand why you'd just disappear like that."

"Zeph, I'm –"

"I know what you're going to say. It had nothing to do with me; it's just how you react to make things hurt less. I get it. But for nights after you left, I'd sit here alone and have imaginary conversations with you. You'd tell me how much happier you were since you left, and how you wished that you'd done it sooner. Whenever I asked you if you missed me or if you regretted not saying goodbye, you'd pause a little longer than necessary and tell me 'of course I do, Zeph'. Your voice would always sound so nonchalant in my head. It tore me apart."

She flicks ash into the Milo can and misses. I stay in the silence, leaving it entirely up to her to fill with words that she has been waiting to say.

"Some days I didn't miss you as much. I took it as a sign that I was healing, that I finally stopping tripping over something that was already behind me. Then 'Love and Happiness' would play on one of my Spotify playlists, or Mid-Autumn festival comes by, or someone would use your name in a sentence and I'd just – "

Zephyr lets out a shuddering breath and laughs dryly. "It could even be something like, 'Will you join us?' and I'd involuntarily wince. When I lost you, I felt like I lost a part of myself. I started doing things that kept me distracted, that helped to ignore the ache."

She falls silent and I look into her eyes. She shakes her head and reaches over to open the packet of wheel crackers. "Don't feel bad, I didn't do anything excessive. I was just casually dating around for a while. They were all fun and charming but not the type of men that I'd settle down with. It just felt easier, you know? For the longest time, love was the last thing on my mind. I did not want to expect it from anyone. It seemed selfish. I enjoyed having no expectations. Then Sebastian came along and ruined everything."

She pours a handful of wheel crackers into her palm and offers the bag to me like an olive branch. I take it from her.

"I didn't think that I'd settle down with him," she says. "Not that I'm saying he isn't my type. He's warm, quiet and sincere, cares about the little things instead of the grand gestures, adores our differences and marvels at our similarities. He comes across a little strange at times but he's my kind of strange. Do you know what I mean?"

"Yes I do."

"But I was still rediscovering myself and wanted to keep it that way. I enjoyed the fact that I was alone. I wanted to go to an airport, stand in front of the digital flight board, pick a random destination and just go. But Sebastian really fought to keep me in his life. He was patient yet determined, always finding ways to prove his love. Whenever I tried to laugh things off and deflect, he made sure to address whatever he thought I was feeling. And he was almost always right."

"So when did he propose?"

"Funnily enough, it was on the day we became official that he told me that he wanted to marry me. I jokingly told him that if we made it through three years without him getting tired of me, I'd accept. Exactly three years from that day he popped the question."

I set the bag of snacks next to me. "He sounds like a great guy," I say.

"He is. He's very sweet to me. He tells me everything. Every silly little thing he feels, he just blurts it out like he can't help it."

She notices my reaction and her dreamy smile quickly fades away. "I'm sorry, I'm being insensitive."

"Please don't say that. I'm genuinely happy for you."

"Don't hide what you're feeling, Will."

"I'm not going to hide anything from you anymore, Zeph," I say, meeting her curious gaze. I cannot tell if it is just my imagination but I feel the earth beneath us quietly begin to shift. That shouldn't be possible.

"I couldn't bear to say goodbye to you," I finally explain. "Deep down I knew that if I saw you again, I wouldn't be able to leave. So, I flew off without saying a word, as an act of moving on, of cowardice. But I never moved forward. You have been in the back of my mind for every single day for the past seven years. The entire time I was in Melbourne, I never felt truly close to anyone. Even when I wasn't alone, I was lonely. I guess I've always been a lonely person. But I don't feel lonely at all when I'm with you."

She opens her mouth to speak but I already know what she wants to say, so I save her from the need to comfort me. "I know what I did was wrong. I shouldn't have taken so long to let you know how much you mean to me. I shouldn't have been so trapped in my own head, uncomfortable in my own skin, foolishly spending years trying to escape from myself. I'm not going to run anymore. I shouldn't have pushed you away when you're the one who I keep closest. I did a terrible thing to you, Zephyr. I'm really sorry."

Zephyr nods. "I forgive you, Will."

I start to cry. It has been so long since I last cried that I am surprised that my tear ducts are still operational after lack of use. But here I am, positively bawling. She cradles my insecurities and holds me close as I look up at my best friend through blurred vision, overwhelmed by all that I failed to express. But Zephyr knows. She always knows.

"You mean so much to me," Zephyr says, amidst my choking sobs as I try to steady my breathing. "I love every word you say to me and every look you give. You make me feel recognised."

"Zephyr."

This entire time, her left hand and my right hand rest in what little space we have between us, fingers hovering near each other as though dancing. She reaches over and entwines her fingers with mine, raising our locked hands to her face. She rubs it against her cheek, smiling to herself. There's something about the way she does this that makes me feel like crying again. It is as though she's making sure I won't suddenly disappear.

"I'm not going to leave you again," I say and she looks at me. "I'd like to grow old with you. I know that you used to say that in the past, and I would brush it aside because a part of me always felt that I did not deserve you. But I recognise that I do deserve good in my life. Which is exactly what you are. So I'd like to be a part of your world in any capacity that you'd let me. Whether it's organising your bridal shower, being in charge of floral arrangements, parking cars at the wedding... babysitting your kids, teaching your grandchildren the importance of grammar and punctuation... whatever you and Sebastian, your soon-to-be husband, need, however I can help you lighten any load and bring you joy. I'd like to be there. I know it's not possible for me to make up for what I did to you. But for the rest of my life I'm going to try."

I can see her eyes beginning to water. She smiles at me like I have never seen her smile before.

"Why weren't we endgame, Will?" she asks.

I smile back at my best friend, stroking her cheek affectionately. She feels both cool and warm to my fingertips. "We are endgame, Zeph. It doesn't have to be romantic to be real. I used to think that love was this... unfathomable concept that scientists and mathematicians could not formulate. Sometimes, I'd even believe it was fictional. But now, I've come to understand its definition. It's the way that I feel about you. It is you who makes this life electric."

She really is crying now. "You're not going to leave me again."

"Never."

"Because you recognise me."

"And you recognise me too."

After all these years, I have never seen such tenderness in Zephyr's eyes, her face playing a symphony.

"...And I'm your favourite song."

I feel happier than I ever have been. I am burning up from my best friend's radiance as she glows brighter than anything I have ever seen.

"You're my favourite song," I say.